Percival Frost

Materials for Latin Prose

Percival Frost

Materials for Latin Prose

ISBN/EAN: 9783337371036

Printed in Europe, USA, Canada, Australia, Japan

Cover: Foto ©Andreas Hilbeck / pixelio.de

More available books at **www.hansebooks.com**

MATERIALS

FOR LATIN PROSE.

BY THE

REV. PERCIVAL FROST, M.A.

LATE FELLOW OF ST. JOHN'S COLLEGE, CAMBRIDGE.

NEW EDITION.

LONDON:

BELL AND DALDY, 186, FLEET STREET.

1866.

MATERIALS FOR

LATIN PROSE COMPOSITION.

—◆—

INTRODUCTION.

As Rome was not built in a day, so the art of writing her language is not to be acquired by reading a short preface or a few rules. In truth, in the acquisition of this skill, there are two distinct stages: he who arrives at the end of the first will be yet far distant from the completion of the second. The first point to aim at is the avoidance of syntactical errors; and to this end rules are available and useful. Experience shows that successive learners run through nearly the same round of mistakes, until one can predict, in any given piece, without much chance of failure, where the error will intrude. Of course there are exceptions to this, and perverse ingenuity will always find 'ample room and verge enough,' and new worlds to conquer. Still, in the main, the errors of those who have recently left the usual exercise books can be reduced to a few heads. To prevent mistakes in these respects, I have written down a few leading principles, an observance of which will purify the composition of learners from the more glaring faults, and bring them tolerably well to the end of the first stage. To attain to the end of the second, and write not only without errors, but also with some moderate degree of elegance and taste, is of course a work of time and patient diligence. Practice and lengthened acquaintance with the classical authors, the pure wells of Latin undefiled, are necessary to this end. Perhaps the passages quoted in the notes may be of some use at times in bringing before the learner many idioms of the language ; but a close observance of the authors he reads for himself will be of much more. First, then,

I. A proper sequence of tenses is most carefully to be observed in Latin composition.

When the main verb of a sentence is in the *present* or *future* tense, the dependent conjunctive verb, denoting object or result, must be in the *present:* ex. *Quis vult omnibus copiis circumfluere, ut not diligat quenquam?* 'Who wishes to have abundance, on condition of loving no one ?'

When the main verb is in the *past,* the dependent conjunctive verb is in the *imperfect : Dixit se non adduci posse ut hoc crederet à Biante esse dictum,* ' He said that he could not induce himself to believe this to have been asserted by Bias.' The only violation of this rule is afforded by the construction of an historic present with past dependent verbs; from the principle, that an historic present really describes a past event.

A perfect conjunctive points out time anterior to a main verb in the present : *Ei gratias agit quod de se optimum judicium fecerit,* ' He thanks him for having thought so highly of him.'

A pluperfect conjunctive points out time anterior to a main verb in the past : *Ei gratias egit quod de se optimum judicium fecisset,* ' He thanked him for having thought so highly of him.'

A present infinitive points out time contemporary with that of the main verb in whatever tense the main verb is put : *Dixit eum collocare matrem homini nobilissimo,* ' He said that he was *then* betrothing his mother to an eminent man.'

A perfect infinitive points out time anterior to that of the main verb, in whatever tense the main verb is put : *Dicit* or *dixit eum collocasse matrem,* ' He says, or said, that he had *previously* betrothed his mother.'

II. An inconsiderate rendering of the English word " to," denoting purpose, leads to numerous errors. When two verbs are connected by the word " to," and the latter describes the result or purpose of the former, the latter verb must *not* be constructed in the infinitive mood. The conjunctive with *ut,* or the preposition *ad* with the gerundive in *dus,* or some equivalent construction, must be employed. For instance, ' he sent ambassadors to sue for peace,' can never be translated *legatos misit pacem petere,* because the suing for peace is the *object* of sending the ambassadors : it must be either *legatos misit ut* or *qui peterent,* or *ad pacem petendam,* or *pacis petendæ causâ,* or *pacem petitum.* A gerund governing the case of its verb is not so usual as the gerundive agreeing with the noun :

ex. *pacem petendi causâ* is not so common as *pacis petendæ causâ*, unless it prevent ambiguity.

The following verbs, however, do take the succeeding verb in the infinitive, although connected by the word " to," viz. : *cupio, volo, nolo, malo, pergo, conor, desino, jubeo ;* and the passives of all verbs of calling, asserting, &c.

III. Any verb conveying a positive *assertion* that any thing is, or will be, or has been actually done, or has taken place, takes the succeeding verb in the infinitive : ex. *Legionem urgeri ab hoste vidisset,*' He saw that the legion was hard pressed by the enemy.'

Consequently all verbs of warning, reminding, persuading, and the like, have double constructions : when used in the sense of warning, &c. a man to do a thing, they take, by the last rule, a conjunctive with *ut*, denoting the purpose of the warning, &c. : *Moneo te ut hoc facias*, 'I warn you to do this.' When used in the sense of warning or reminding a man that something has been done, they are constructed like words of asserting, and so take the infinitive : *Moneo te hoc factum esse*, 'I remind you that this has been done.'

IV. In describing or narrating the words or thoughts of another, depending on a verb of assertion, as *dico, narro,* or the like, the principal verbs are put in the infinitive by the preceding rule, and the dependent verbs, in clauses beginning with relatives or conjunctions, are put in the conjunctive mood. This is called the "oratio obliqua."

Ex. *Dixit hos multitudinem deterrere ne frumentum conferant quod præstare debeant,* 'He said that they deterred the commonalty from contributing the corn they are bound to supply.' Consequently, if in a narrative of another's words or sentiments any verbs in dependent sentences are in the indicative, they represent the sentiments not of the person whose words are recorded, but of the historian who is writing the narrative, and are in fact parenthetic explanations for the benefit of the reader.

V. All words that can be used in a direct question, such as *quis, qualis, quantus,* &c., when used in subsidiary sentences, depending immediately on another verb, require the conjunctive mood : ex. *Quis es,* 'Who are you?' but *Scio quis sis,* 'I know who you are.'

The conjunctive mood is also required after the relative *qui,* when it in any way assigns a reason : *Odi eum qui dixerit,* 'I hate him because he says.' Otherwise, when *qui* merely introduces a new descriptive circumstance, the indicative is used : *Scipio, qui eo anno consul fuit, mortuus est,* 'Scipio, who was consul that year, died.'

VI. With respect to the position of words in a sentence, few definite rules can be given, and those only generally true, as particular circumstances may entirely alter the arrangement.

The emphatic positions are at the beginning and the end of the sentence : ex. *Civem Romanum verberari nefas est,* where the man's citizenship is the important point. The verb generally being the most important word in the sentence is placed at the end : *Convivium ad multam noctem vario sermone producimus.*

The governing word generally comes after the word governed : *vitæ satietas* is far more common than *satietas vitæ.*

The adjective follows the noun with which it agrees : *ver bonus, pater suus.*

ENGLISH SELECTIONS.

I.

Now the land belonged to a people, who were the children of the soil,[1] and their king was called Latinus. He received the strangers kindly, and granted to them seven hundred jugera of land, seven jugera [2] to each man, for that was a man's portion. But soon the children of the soil and the strangers quarrelled; and the strangers plundered the lands round about them; and King Latinus called upon Turnus, the king of the Rutulians of Ardea, to help him against them. The quarrel became a war;[3] and the strangers took the city of King Latinus. and Latinus was killed; and Æneas took his daughter Lavinia and married her, and became king over the children of the soil; and they and the strangers became one people, and they were called by one name, Latins.

ARNOLD's History of Rome, chap. i.

II.

The two brothers did not wish to live at Alba, but loved rather the hill on the banks of the Tiber, where

---

[1] *children of the soil.* Use 'aborigines.' Avoid employing the conjunction 'et' to connect the clauses too frequently: such a sentence as 'urbem adortus est, et cepit, et regem interfecit' is inelegant; instead of 'quum urbem oppugnatam cepisset, regem interfecit,' or a similar turn.

[2] *seven jugera.* Use the distributive form 'septenus:' 'septem' could only mean they had seven amongst them.

[3] *The quarrel became a war.* Turn by 'out of the quarrel arose a war,' or 'a war having arisen, when the strangers,' &c.

they had been brought up.[1] So they said that they would
build a city there ; and they inquired of the gods by
augury, to know which of them should give his name to
the city.   They watched the heavens [2] from morning till
evening, and from evening till morning, and, as the sun
was rising, Remus saw six vultures.   This was told to
Romulus ; but as they were telling him, behold there
appeared to him twelve vultures.   Then it was disputed [3]
again,[4] which had seen the truest sign of the god's favour,
but the most part gave their voices to Romulus.

ARNOLD'S *Rome*, chap. i.

III.

So he began to build his city on the Palatine Hill.
This made Remus very angry,[5] and when he saw the ditch
and the rampart which were drawn round the space
where the city was to be, he scornfully leapt over them,
saying, "Shall such defences as these keep your city?"[6] As
he did this, Celer, who had the charge of the building,[7]
struck Remus with the spade [8] which he held in his hand,
and slew him; and they buried him on the hill Remuria, by
the banks of the Tiber,[9] on the spot where he had wished
to build his city.   ARNOLD'S *Rome*, chap. i.

[1] For the first sentence cf. Æn.
i. 15, 16. 'Quàm Juno . . . . post-
habitâ coluisse Samo.'

[2] *They watched the heavens*, &c.
Cf. Æn. vi. 579 : turn by an abla-
tive absolute, or by 'quum' with
a subjunctive; to avoid a succession
of verbs connected by ' et.'

[3] *it was disputed*. Cf. ' de jure
publico disceptaretur armis.'

[4] *again*. 'Iterùm' should be used
here, not 'rursus:' the former means
a *second* time : the latter again
after any previous number of times.

[5] *This made Remus*, &c.   Turn
by ' Remus, being angry, when
he had seen,' &c.

[6] *Shall such defences*, &c.   Turn
this by an indirect question, instead
of a direct one ; the former being
more usual : not ' dicens, Ea ne
mœnia urbem defendent,' but
'quærens ea ne mœnia urbem de-
fensura essent.'

[7] *had charge of the building*.
Cf. Ov. Fasti iv. 837, 'Hoc Celer
urget opus,' or 'qui mœnia ædifi-
canda curabat.'

[8] *A spade*—'rutrum' (Ov. Fasti
iv. 843).

[9] *Bury by the banks of the Tiber*.
Cf. Liv. i. 2, 'Super flumen Numi-
cium situs est.'

IV.

But Romulus found that his people were too few[1] in numbers; so he set apart a place of refuge, to which any man might flee, and be safe from his pursuers. So many fled thither from the countries round about; those who had shed blood[2] and fled from the vengeance of the avenger of blood;[3] those who were driven out from their own homes by their enemies; and even men of low degree,[4] who had run away from their lords. Thus the city became full of people; but yet they wanted wives, and the nations round about would not give them their daughters in marriage. So Romulus gave out that he was going to keep a great festival, and there were to be sports and games to draw a multitude together. The neighbours came to see the show with their wives and their daughters; there came the people of Cænina, and of Crustumerium, and of Antemna, and a great multitude of the Sabines. But while they were looking at the games,[5] the people of Romulus rushed out upon them, and carried off the women to be their wives.

V.

There is a hill near to the Tiber which was divided from the Palatine Hill by a low and swampy valley; and on this hill Romulus made a fortress, to keep off[6] the enemy from his city. But when the fair Tarpeia,[7] the daughter of the chief who had charge of the fortress, saw the

---

[1] *too few.* Use the comparative 'paucior:' which either means fewer than others, or fewer than usual, or fewer than is right, that is, 'too few.' Turn the first sentence, 'Romulus, thinking his people too few, set apart,' &c.

[2] *shed blood.* Use 'cædem facere,' or 'homicidium facere.'

[3] *An avenger of blood,* 'ultor parricidii.'

[4] *men of low degree.* Cf. Sall. in Catil. 23, 'haud obscuro loco natus.'

[5] *looking at the games.* Cf. Liv. i. 9, 'ubi spectaculi tempus venit deditæque eò mentes cum oculis erant.'

[6] *to keep off.* The supine cannot be used here, because there is no verb of motion: in the last exercise, 'They come to see' might be 'spectatum veniunt.'

[7] *the fair Tarpeia.* 'Tarpeia virgo formosa,' or 'pulcherrima.' Adjectives do not seem to be used much with proper names alone.

Sabines draw near, and marked their bracelets and their
collars of gold, she longed after these ornaments, and
promised to betray the hill into their hands if they would
give her those things which they wore upon their arms.[1]
So she opened a gate and let in the Sabines ; and they, as
they came in, threw upon her their shields which they
bore on their arms, and crushed her to death.[2]

ARNOLD'S *Rome*, chap. i.

VI.

After this they fought again [3] in the valley, and the
people of Romulus were beginning to flee, when Romulus
prayed to Jove, the stayer of flight,[4] that he might stay
the people ; and so their flight was stayed, and they turned
again to the battle.   And now the fight was fiercer than
ever, when, on a sudden, the Sabine women who had been
carried off, ran down the hill Palatinus, and ran in between
their husbands and their fathers,[5] and prayed them to
lay aside their quarrel.   So they made peace with one
another,[6] and the two people became as one.

ARNOLD'S *Rome*, chap. i.

VII.

At last, after he had reigned nearly forty years, it
chanced that [7] one day he called his people together in the
field of Mars, near the Goat's Pool,[8] when, all on a sudden,
there arose a dreadful storm, and all was as dark as night ;
and the rain and thunder and lightning were so terrible

[1] *if they would give her,* &c.
Turn by ' having bargained for
what they wore.' Cf. Liv. i. 11,
' pepigisse eam quod in sinistris
manibus haberent.'

[2] *To crush any one to death,* 'qm
obrutum necare.'

[3] *they fought again.* Cf. Liv. i.
13, 'prœlium redintegrant.'

[4] *Jove, the stayer of flight.* Use
' Jupiter Stator.'

[5] *ran in between,* &c. Turn, 'a

rush being made across, on the one
hand prayed their husbands, on
the other their fathers,' &c.

[6] *they made peace,* &c.   Turn by
a single sentence, ' peace being
made,' &c. and cf. Liv. i. 13, 'civitatem unam ex duabus faciunt.'

[7] *it chanced that.*   Use ' forte
concionem habere,' or ' forte accidit
ut,' &c.

[8] *near the Goat's Pool,* ' ad
capræ paludem.'

that all the people fled from the field and ran to their several homes.[1]   At last the storm was over, and they came back to the field of Mars, but Romulus was nowhere to be found;[2] for Mars, his father, had carried him up to heaven in his chariot.[3]   ARNOLD'S *Rome*, chap. i.

VIII.

Tullus was a warlike king, and he soon was called to prove his valour;[4] for the countrymen[5] of the Alban border and of the Roman border plundered one another. Now Alba was governed by Caius Cluilius, who was the dictator; and Cluilius sent to Rome to complain of the wrongs done to his people, and Tullus sent to Alba for the same purpose.   So there was a war between the two nations, and Cluilius led his people against Rome, and lay encamped within five miles[6] of the city, and there he died. Mettius Fufetius was then chosen dictator in his room,[7] and as the Albans still lay in their camp, Tullus passed them by, and marched into the land of Alba.[8]

ARNOLD'S *Rome*, chap. i.

IX.

The Albans were now bound[9] to obey the Romans : and Tullus called upon them to aid him in a war against the

[1] *ran to their several homes.* Uso 'passim diffugere.'

[2] *was nowhere to be found.* Cf. Lucrot. vi. 1218, 'nec tamen omnino temere ollis solibus ulla comparebat avis.'

[3] *in his chariot.* Cf. Hor. iii. 3, 'Martis equis Acheronta fugit.' In phrases like 'so terrible that,' 'adeo,' 'ita' and the like must be followed by 'ut' with the subjunctive, not by the infinitive. Cf. Tac. Hist. i. 3. 'non adeo sterile virtutum sæculum ut non et bona exempla prodiderit.' Observe also that when 'ut' means 'as' or 'when,' it takes the indicative mood; when it means 'in order that' or 'although,' it takes the subjunctive.

[4] *called to prove his valour.* Cf.

Cic. ad Q. Frat. i. 2, 'edere exemplum severitatis, 'also, 'documentum facere.'

[5] *for the countrymen.* Turn by 'for the Alban countrymen plundered from the Roman land, and the Roman from the Alban,' and uso 'invicem prædas agere.'

[6] *within five miles.* Observe the form, 'haud amplius quinque,' with the 'quàm' omitted ; so, 'haud amplius ducenti erant.'

[7] *chosen dictator in his room.* Cf. Liv. v. 31, 'in ejus locum Cornelius suffectus est.'

[8] *land of Alba.* Uso 'ager Romanus,' not 'ager Romæ.'

[9] *were now bound.* Cf. 'Principum munus est resistere levitati multitudinis.'

people of Veii [1] and Fidenæ.   But in the battle, the Alban
leader, Mettius Fufetius, stood aloof, and gave no true aid
to the Romans.   So when the Romans had won the battle,
Tullus called the Albans together as if he were going to
make a speech to them ; and they came to hear him, as
was the custom, without their arms; and the Roman soldiers
gathered round them, and they could neither fight nor
escape.   Then Tullus took Mettius and bound him between
two chariots, and drove the chariots different ways, [2] and
tore him asunder.   After this he sent his people to Alba,
and they destroyed the city and made all the Albans come
and live at Rome.

ARNOLD's *Rome*, chap. i.

X.

Ancient story does not tell much of Ancus Marcius.
He published the religious ceremonies which Numa had
commanded, and had them written out upon whited
boards, [3] and hung up round the forum, that all might
know and observe them. [4]   He had a war with the Latins
and conquered them, and brought the people to Rome,
and gave them the hill Aventinus to dwell on.   He
founded a colony at Ostia by the mouth of the Tiber.
He built a fortress on the hill Janiculum, and joined the
hill to the city by a wooden bridge [5] over the river.   He
secured the city in the low grounds [6] between the hills by
a great dyke, which was called the dyke of the Quirites.
And he built a prison under the hill Saturnius towards
the forum, because, as the people grew in numbers,

[1] *people of Veii.* Observe that
in a phrase like this, the plural of
'populus' is not to be used, which
implies a collection of different
tribes or peoples : also avoid 'populus Veiorum,' ' populus Romæ'
and the like, but turn by the adjective, 'populus Veiens,' and so on.
The same rule applies to such
phrases as ' a citizen of Rome,'
&c. which must be rendered by
' civis Romanus.'

[2] *drove the chariots different
ways.* Use ' equi in diversum (iter)

concitati.'

[3] *had them written out,* &c. Cf.
Liv.i.32, 'in album relata in publico
proponi jubet.' ' To have anything
done' is ' qd faciendum curare.'

[4] *that all might observe them.* Cf.
Liv. v. 13, 'promiscuoque usu omnium in propatulo posito.' Livy
also uses ' in propatulis.'

[5] *wooden bridge.* Use ' pons
sublicius.'

[6] *in the low grounds.* Cf. Liv. i.
32, ' à planioribus aditu locis.'

offenders against the laws became more numerous also. At last king Ancus died after a reign of three-and-twenty years. ARNOLD'S *Rome*, chap. i.

XI.

But Tarquinius was in great favour with [1] the people; and when he desired to be king, they resolved to choose him rather than the sons of Ancus. So he began to reign, and he did great works [2] both in war and peace. He made war on the Latins and took from them a great spoil. Then he made war on the Sabines, and he conquered them in two battles,[3] and took from them the town of Collatia, and gave it to Egerius, his brother's son, who had come with him from Tarquinii. Lastly, there was another war with the Latins, and Tarquinius went round to their cities, and took them one after another; for none dared to go out to meet him in open battle.[4]

ARNOLD'S *Rome*, chap. iv.

XII.

The labour, which is not great, will hereafter be a great honour to you.[5] By that path which you are now entering, many who were born in an humble and obscure station [6] have arrived at the highest dignities. And even if no such rewards were proposed for literature, yet learning of itself would deserve to be loved: [7] and nothing is more disgraceful in a freeborn man than ignorance of those things, a knowledge of which cannot be acquired without literature. The pleasure which is derived from disgraceful things

---

[1] *To be in great favour with,* 'Apud qm gratiosum esse,' or 'gratiam apud qm inire,' or 'es gratiâ florere.'

[2] *To do great works.* Cf. Liv. i. 16, 'his immortalibus operibus editis.'

[3] *conquered them in two battles.* Cf. Livy's phrase, 'geminâ victoriâ superaro.'

[4] *To meet in open battle.* Cf. Liv. i. 38, 'nusquam ad universæ rei dimicationem ventum est.' Also,

'in acie dimicare.'

[5] *a great honour to you.* Cf. Cic. de Off. ii. 17, 'honori summo nostro Miloni fuit.' Several other words are thus used in the dative: 'auxilium,' 'subsidium,' 'laus,' 'exitium,' 'damnum,' &c.

[6] *born in a humble station.* See Ex. IV.

[7] *deserve to be loved.* Either 'dignum esse qui ametur,' or 'dignum esse amore.'

quickly passes away, but leaves a lasting pain on the mind ; but labour bestowed on honourable objects, itself, indeed, disappears, but leaves a remembrance of itself in the mind full of the noblest and purest pleasure. Think of these things,[1] and farewell.

XIII.

Now he first had it in his mind to make three new centuries of horsemen, and to call them after his own name. But Attus Navius, who was greatly skilled in augury, forbade him. Then the king mocked at[2] his art, and said, " Come now, thou augur, tell me by thy auguries whether the thing which I now have in my mind may be done or not." And Attus asked counsel of the gods by augury, and he answered, " It may." Then the king said, " It was in my mind[3] that thou shouldest cut in two this whetstone with this razor : take them and do it, and fulfil thy augury." But Attus took the razor and cut the whetstone asunder. So the king obeyed his counsels, and made no new centuries.   ARNOLD'S *Rome*, chap. iv.

XIV.

After this Tullus made war upon the Sabines, and gained a victory over them. But now, whether it were that[4] Tullus had neglected the worship of the gods, whilst he had been so busy in his wars, the signs of the wrath of

---

[1] *Think of these things.* Cf. Cic. ad Att. ix. 6, ' ad hæc cogita :' ' ad hæc,' ' hæc,' and ' de his cogitare,' are all found.

[2] *To mock at,* 'ludibrio habere.' Cf. 'ludibrio pessima me habuisti,' Plaut. Cas. III. v. 26; or 'eludere ;' cf. Liv. i. 36, 'ex eo ira regi mota, eludensque artem,' &c.

[3] *It was in my mind.* Turn either by the oratio directa, as in the English, or by the oratio obliqua, ' the king said that it was in his mind,' &c. In the latter case, 'take them and do it' must be put in the imperfect subjunctive, which is the oratio obliqua of the imperative. Cf. Tac. Hist. i. 32, 'non eundum ad iratos censebat : daret malorum pœnitentiæ spatium.' Also Liv. i. 9, ' illas in societate fore ; mollirent iras,' &c.

[4] *whether it were that.* This is not to be turned by ' sive,' which can only be used when two or more things are mentioned, as 'sive casu, sive consilio deorum,' Cæs. B. Gall. i. 12, but by ' forte quin,' or a similar phrase.

heaven became manifest—a plague broke out among the people, and Tullus himself was at last stricken with a lingering disease.[1] Then he bethought him of good and holy Numa, and how in his time the gods had been so gracious to Rome, and had made known their will by signs whenever Numa inquired of them. So Tullus also tried to inquire [2] of Jupiter; but the god was angry and sent his lightnings, and Tullus and all his house were burnt to ashes. This made the Romans know that they wanted a king who would follow the example of Numa; so they chose his daughter's son, Ancus Marcius, to reign over them in the room of [3] Tullus.

ARNOLD's Rome, chap. i.

XV.

He was seized and brought before the king, and the guards threatened him with sharp torments [4] unless he would answer all their questions. But he said, "See how little I care for your torments;" and he thrust his right hand into the fire that was burning there on the altar. Then king Porsenna marvelled at his courage, and said, "Go thy way, for thou hast harmed thyself more than me; and thou art a brave man, and I send thee back to Rome unhurt and free. But Caius answered, "For this thou shalt get more of my secret than thy tortures could have forced from me. Three hundred noble youths [5] of Rome have bound themselves by oath to take thy life. Mine was the first adventure; [6] but the others will each in his turn lie in wait for thee: I warn thee therefore to look well to thyself." Then Caius was let go, and went back again into the city.

ARNOLD's Rome, chap. vii.

[1] *To be stricken with a lingering disease.* 'Longinquo morbo implicari;' cf. Liv. i. 31, or ' morbo diuturno tabescere.' (Cic.)

[2] *tried to inquire.* Cf. Liv. ix. 20, ' quum fatigassent singulos precibus.'

[3] *To choose in the room of.* Sce Ex. VIII.

[4] *threatened him with torments.* "arn by ' threatened torments to nim.' Cf. Cic. pro Planc. 40, 'deflagrationem urbi minabatur.'

[5] *Three hundred youths.* As Caius includes himself, the verb must be in the first person plural, ' trecenti conjuravimus.'

[6] *adventure.* ' sors.'

XVI.

See how I love you:[1] though I have received letters to
day from many persons, I thought I ought to do nothing
before I answered you in preference to all the rest.[2] Do
not think, my Alexander, that you are dearer to your
father than to me. And if you should ask [3] what is the
cause of this great love of mine towards you, may I die if [4]
I can assign any other than that I think I have discovered
in you excellent talents, and if you choose to employ them,
adapted by nature for the highest things. But do you
reflect on this; that there are many things in their own
nature indeed good, but which sometimes become very bad
and pernicious by the fault of those who possess them.

XVII.

Wealth is good; but if any one does not use it aright,
bad. Comeliness is a good thing; yet this good thing
has proved the destruction of many. Of the same kind is
talent : if you use it aright, scarcely any greater or more
excellent gift can be bestowed on the human race ; but if
to good talent a bad disposition is joined, it will be the
same thing as a sword in the hand of a madman—the
better and sharper it is, the more mischief it will produce.[5]
I love you now because you have good talents. I shall
cease to love you, if you begin [6] to use your talents to a
bad purpose; but I hope this will not be, and I trust that
you will use them well, both of your own inclination, and

[1] *See how I love you,* vid. Introd.
V.

[2] *I thought I ought to do,* &c.
Turn by 'I thought the rest to be
postponed to you.' Cf. Virg. Ecl.
vii. 17, 'Posthabui tamen illorum
mea seria ludo,' or cf. Cic. ad Att.
iv. 1, 'Nihil prius faciendum putavi
quàm ut tibi gratularer.'

[3] *if you should ask.* Turn by
the present, not the imperfect,
which would not suit the present
form of the rest of the sentence.

[4] *may I die if.* Cf. Cic. Epist. xv.
19, 'peream nisi sollicitus sum.'

Also cf. Cic. ad Att. iv. 16, 'ne
vivam si scio.'

[5] *the better and sharper.* Turn
by 'quo'—'eo,' or 'quanto'—
'tanto.'—Sometimes 'tanto' is
omitted.   Cf. Tac. Hist. iii. 18,
'Propinqua mœnia quanto plus
spei ad effugium, minorem ad re-
sistendum animum dabant.' But
they cannot be both omitted.

[6] *if you begin.* As the whole
action contemplated is future, and
yet this portion of it is anterior to
the 'ceasing to love,' 'begin' must
be in the second future.

because you seem greatly to like my affection for you, which you cannot preserve in any other way. Farewell; and if you love me, love virtue and learning : there are no greater blessings belonging to men. Once more, farewell.

XVIII.

The Veientians dared not meet the Romans in the open field ;[1] but they troubled them exceedingly with their incursions to plunder the country. And on the other side the Æquians and the Volscians were making war upon the Romans year after year ; and while one consul ♥ went to 2 fight with the Æquians and the other with the Volscians, there was no one to stop the plunderings of the Veientians. So the men of the Fabian house[3] consulted together ; and when they had resolved what to do, they all went to the senate-house. And Kœso Fabius, who was consul for that year, went into the senate and said, " We of the house of the Fabii take upon us to fight with the Veientians.[4] We ask neither men nor money from the commonwealth ; but we will wage war with our own bodies at ōur own cost." The senate heard him joyfully ; and then he went home, and the other men of his house followed him ; and he told them to come to him[5] the next day, each man in his full arms ; and so they departed.

ARNOLD'S *Rome*, chap. x.

XIX.

There is no one to whom I write[6] more willingly than to you ; for I feel quite a fatherly disposition[7] and affec-

[1] *in the open field.* 'Campus' is not to be used in this sense : use 'acie dimicare.'

[2] *one consul.* As this is one of two use 'alter,' not 'alius,' which means one out of many.

[3] *the men of the Fabian house.* Cf. Liv. ii. 48, 'Tum Fabia gens senatum adiit.'

[4] *take upon us to fight.* Cf. 'quæ occidendum virum regnumque adultero tradendum susceperat.'

[5] *told them to come.* As the infinitive never denotes a purpose,

'dixit venire' can only mean 'he told them they were then coming,' and is of course incorrect here. As 'to tell' here means 'to order,' it must take the usual construction of verbs of ordering.

[6] *to whom I write.* Use 'scribero ad qm' or ' ei ;' the former seems more usual, although Cicero has both forms.

[7] *To feel a fatherly disposition.* Use 'paterno esse animo,' cf. Cic. ad Att. i. 3, 'est animo abalienato.'

C

tion towards you. But you can scarcely believe how much I am occupied in this retirement, which, however, all believe to be full of leisure ; and I receive every day five or six letters [1] from my friends, all of which [2] if I attempted to answer, I must do nothing else. It is agreeable to me that you have cultivated the acquaintance of Æmilius and Macaranus, for both of them may improve you both by instruction and example. To such men attach yourself ; but avoid like a pestilence the society of those who are of a different disposition. At your age, nothing requires to be more carefully attended to than what company you keep. I do not, however, wish you to be rigid and sullen, and an enemy [3] to every kind of pleasure. I only suggest this, that not those friendships should be sought which seem most agreeable ; but that the mind should be brought to think [4] those which are most honourable are also the most agreeable and delightful. Farewell again and again.

XX.

Massinissa was the son of Gala, and when very young, at the head of his father's army, gave a most signal overthrow [5] to Syphax, then an ally of the Romans. Soon after, Asdrubal gave the beautiful Sophonisba, his daughter, in marriage to the young prince. But this marriage was not consummated, on account of Massinissa's being obliged to hasten into Spain, there to command his father's troops. The affairs of the Carthaginians at this time began to be in a bad condition, and they thought it might be greatly for

---

[1] *five or six letters.* Cf. Cic. Epist. x. 18, ' quum binis litteris ut venirem rogaret,' and Cic. ad Att. ii. 12, ' O suaves epistolas tuas, uno tempore mihi datas, duas !' With ' litterae,' the forms ' binae,' 'ternae,' ' quaternae,' &c. must be used : ' duae litterae' would mean two letters of the alphabet.

[2] *all of which.* Put ' omnis' in the same case as the relative.

[3] *an enemy to pleasure.* ' Inimicus,' not ' hostis ;' this last generally means a public enemy. Cf.

De leg. Man. x., ' qui saepius cum hoste conflixit quam quisquam cum inimico concertavit.'

[4] *the mind should be brought to think.* Cf. Liv. xxvii. 9, ' quod ut pronuntiarent in animum inducere non possent ;' and Cic. Tusc. v. 10, ' inducant animum opes contemnere.'

[5] *To give a signal overthrow.* ' Praeclarè qm vincere,' or ' gloriosam victoriam consequi' (Cic. pro Cæl. vii.), or ' reportare,' or ' referre.'

their interest if they could bring over Syphax to themselves. This, in time, they actually effected, and to strengthen the new alliance, commanded Asdrubal to give his daughter to Syphax. She was accordingly married to Syphax, and Massinissa, enraged at the affront, became a friend to the Romans. They drove the Carthaginians before them [1] out of Spain, and carried the war into Africa, defeated Syphax, and took him prisoner. The rest of the affair, the marriage, and the sending of the poison, everybody knows. GRAY.

XXI.

Such was the covetousness of the richer sort at this time in England,[2] that they converted many large corn-fields into pastures; hereof ensued a general decay,[3] not only of horses, but of persons who should do their king and country service. Besides sheep, cattle, and clothes oeing thus within the hands of a few, the price was much enhanced.[4] To remedy this mischief, the king caused the statutes provided ou that behalf to be looked into.

XXII.

The Volscians were glad of the arrival of a Roman who was ready to assist them in their wars against Rome; and Attus Tullius, the most distinguished amongst them, and the most inveterate enemy of the Romans, received him hospitably into his house.[5] There was at that time no war with the Volscians, but, as the Romans commanded all Volscians who happened to be staying amongst them forthwith to quit the city, the indignation of the Volscians

---

[1] *They drove the Carthaginians,* &c. Turn by the ablatives of the passive participles.

[2] *Such was the covetousness that.* See Ex. VII.; on 'so terrible that.'

[3] *hereof ensued,* &c. Turn by 'whence not only not horses, but not even men were sufficient,' &c.; and observe that 'not only not,' followed by 'no quidem,' is often rendered by 'non modo,' omitting

the second 'non.' Cf. Cic. Off. iii. 19, 'talis vir non modo facere sed ne cogitare quidem audebit.' Observe also that 'ne' and 'quidem' are separated.

[4] *price was enhanced.* 'Annona carior erat,' or 'crevit.'

[5] *received him hospitably.* Cf. Liv. i. 1, 'apud Latinum Æneam fuisse in hospitio;' or 'hospitio accipere.'

c 2

was roused, and war decreed at once. Coriolanus marched
against Circeii ; he expelled the Roman colonists from the
place, and delivered up the town into the hands of the
Volscians. In like manner he took a great number of
other towns, steadily [1] advancing towards Rome. At length
he pitched his camp near the Cluilian ditch, and ravaged
the country in the vicinity of Rome.[2] The plebeians were
unwilling to fight, and the senate at length resolved to
send ambassadors to Coriolanus, to prevail upon him to
desist from his hostility against his country.   Schmitz.

XXIII.

But they were haughtily received, and sent back with
a scornful answer. A second embassy was not admitted
into the camp ; and it was in vain that even the priests,
attired in their sacred robes, went to him as suppliants.
At length his mother, Veturia, and his wife, Volumnia,
with her two young children, accompanied by many other
Roman matrons, proceeded to the camp of Coriolanus.
What the ambassadors of the senate and the priests of
the gods had been unable to effect was accomplished by
the tears and entreaties of the women. Coriolanus broke
up his camp, and led his legions away from the Roman
territory. Some traditions relate [3] that he died immediately
after, overwhelmed with shame and repentance ; [4] whereas
according to others, he continued to live amongst the
Volscians, and died an old man. The temple of Fortuna
Muliebris is said to have been dedicated in commemoration of the delivery of Rome by the women. Schmitz.

XXIV.

The story runs,[5] that at Athens, once upon a time,
during the celebration of the games, an old gentleman

---

[1] *steadily*, '.agmine composito,'
or perhaps 'pedetentim,' or 'nullâ
intermissione.'

[2] *the country in the vicinity of
Rome.* Use 'ager Romanus.'

[3] *Some traditions relate.* Use

[4] 'alii tradunt,' or 'sunt qui tradant.'

[4] *overwhelmed with shame*, &c.
Cf. Cic. in Pison. xvii., 'oppressus
conscientiâ scelerum.'

[5] *The story runs.* Use 'Memoriæ
proditum est,' or 'narrant.'

considerably advanced in years [1] entered the theatre. Among his countrymen who were present in that large assembly, no one offered him a place. He turned to the Lacedæmonians, who as ambassadors had a certain space allotted them. *They* rose in a body,[2] and begged him to sit amongst them. Loud shouts of applause arose from the whole theatre; whereupon it was remarked, that the Athenians knew their duty,[3] but were slow to exemplify it in their conduct.

XXV.

What youth can say, more than an old man, he shall live till night?[4] Youth catches distempers more easily, its sickness is more violent, and its recovery more doubtful. The youth,[5] indeed, hopes for many more days; so cannot the old man. The youth's hopes are ill-grounded; for what is more foolish than to place any confidence upon an uncertainty? But the old man has not room so much as for hope; he is still happier than the youth; he has already enjoyed what the other does but hope for. One wishes to live long, the other has lived long. But alas, is there anything[6] in human life the durability of which can be called long? There is nothing which must end to be valued for its continuance. If hours, days, months, and years pass away, it is no matter what day, what month, or what year we die. The applause of a good actor is due to him at whatever scene of the play he makes his exit.

SPECTATOR.

[1] *an old gentleman.* Use 'quidam grandis natu,' or 'annis paullò provectior.'

[2] *They rose in a body.* Cf. Cic. in Verr. vi. 62, 'Itaque in curiam venimus: honorificè sanè consurgitur.'

[3] *knew their duty.* Use 'scire quæ recta essent.' For the reason of this subjunctive, see Introd. IV. 'Qui' does not of itself require a subjunctive mood, unless it is put causally for 'ut qui;' as 'maluimus iter facere pedibus qui incommodissimè navigassemus.'

[4] *can say he shall live.* Our idiom allows this omission of 'that,'

but in Latin 'dicit vivet' is wrong: it must be 'dicit se victurum.' So, 'he thinks he shall live' must be either 'credit se victurum,' or 'credit' may sometimes be used parenthetically, as in Cic. De Fin. i. 3, 'male, credo, mererer de meis civibus.'

[5] *The youth.* Observe not to use 'juventus,' which either means 'the period of youth,' or 'a band of youth;' 'the Roman youth,' for instance.

[6] *is there anything.* Cf. Ter. Eun. V. ix. 1, 'Ecquis vivit me fortunatior?'

XXVI.

James hereupon, firing his huts, dislodges covertly by the benefit of the smoke, and keeping still on the high ground,[1] at last he commands a stay. Presently after, the Earl, also traversing some bogs and marshes till he arrived at the bottom of this bank, found the ascent not very steep, and thereupon encourageth his men to fight. This done, he marcheth up;[2] the vanguard was led by his two sons, the battle[3] by himself, and the rear[4] by Stanley; the Lord Dacres, with his horse, being appointed as a reserve on all occasions. He, observing this well, and judging that it was not without disadvantage that the English came to fight, exhorts his men to behave themselves like brave soldiers, and thereupon joins battle.

XXVII.

In the afternoon,[5] the Median and Hyrcanian cavalry rode up, bringing the horses and men whom they had captured. And when they came before him, Cyrus asked them, first, if[6] they themselves were all without harm, then what fortune they had met with. He heard willingly all they related, and then asked them whether they had ridden over much country, and whether it was inhabited. When they said all the country was inhabited, and full of everything, then said he, "We have two things to give

---

[1] *keeping still on the high ground.* Use ' per alta loca iter faciens.'

[2] *he marcheth up.* Cf. Liv. iii. 18, ' In clivum Capitolinum aciem erigunt.'

[3] *the battle;* i. e. 'the main line.' Cf. Liv. xxvii. 48, 'Media acies tuenda datur.'

[4] *the rear.* Cf. Liv. xxxiv. 28, ' equites agmen cogebant.' Observe, in the enumeration of several particulars, to vary if possible the construction of the different clauses: here turn the last clause by ' Stanley brought up the rear.'

[5] *In the afternoon.* Cf. Tac.

Ann. xvi. 34, ' quæstor missus jam vesperascente die.'

[6] *Cyrus asked if.* Observe that ' if' after a verb of asking can never be turned by ' si.' It is when ' if' means ' on the supposition that,' ' in case that,' or the like, that ' si' is the equivalent Latin. Cf. Suet. in Vesp. xxiii., 'sciscitans num odore offenderetur.' Suet. in Vit. vii., ' ut mane singulos jamne jentassent sciscitaretur.' Cf. also the less common form, Liv. xxxvii. 17, ' quum percontatus esset utrumnam classis in portu stare posset.'

heed to, that we may be masters of these inhabitants, and that they may not be driven away ; for a country cleared of its inhabitants is likewise cleared of its wealth."

XXVIII.

Lucius chose Lucius Tarquitus to be master of the horse, a brave man, and of a burgher's house ;[1] but so poor withal, that he had been used to serve among the foot-soldiers[2] instead of among the horse. Then the master of the people and the master of the horse went together into the forum, and bade every man to shut up his booth, and stopped all causes at law,[3] and gave an order that none should look to his own affairs[4] till the consul and his army were delivered from the enemy. They ordered also that every man, who was of an age to go out to battle, should be ready in the field of Mars before sunset, and should have with him victuals for five days and twelve stakes ;[5] and the older men dressed the victuals for the soldiers, whilst the soldiers went about everywhere to get their stakes. So the army was ready in the field of Mars at the time appointed ; and they set forth from the city, and made such haste that ere the night was half spent they came to Algidus ; and when they perceived that they were near the enemy, they made a halt. Then Lucius rode on, and saw how the camp of the enemy lay ; and he ordered his soldiers to throw down all their baggage into one place, but to keep each man his arms and twelve stakes. Then they set out again in their order of march, as they had come from Rome, and they spread themselves round[6] the camp of the enemy on every side.

ARNOLD'S *Rome*, chap. xi.

[1] *of a burgher's house,* 'patriciæ gentis.'

[2] *To serve amongst the foot-soldiers.* Cf. Liv. xxiv. 18, 'ut omnes pedibus mererent ;' or 'pedibus stipendia facere.'

[3] *stopped all causes at law.* Use 'justitium indicere,' or 'edicere.'

[4] *look to his own affairs.* Cf.

Liv. iii. 27, 'quenquam privatæ quicquam rei agere vetat.'

[5] *twelve stakes.* Not 'duodecim,' which would imply that they had twelve stakes amongst them, but 'duodeni,' twelve each.

[6] *spread themselves round.* Cf. Liv. xxii. 14, 'Minucio circumfundebatur multitudo.'

XXIX.

This year the war blazed from its ashes.[1] The Samnites had been obliged to send hostages to Rome, and one of them had escaped to the mountains of his native country, and there gathered round himself a band of robbers and others who had no alternative [2] except a wretched life or cruel death. Two consular armies took the field against the rebels, who had scarcely heard [3] of the approach of the enemy before they gave up the senseless enterprise. The leader of the insurrection was beheaded, the other prisoners sold. In the same year the Picentians revolted against Rome, but were soon conquered, and their whole country reduced to submission. SCHMITZ.

XXX.

When king Pyrrhus was in Italy, and had been conqueror in one or more engagements,[4] and kept the Romans fully employed,[5] and the greater part of Italy had revolted to the king, a certain man of Ambracia, a friend of Pyrrhus, came secretly to Fabricius, asking a reward, for which, if it were given him, he promised to destroy the king by poison ; this, he affirmed,[6] would be easily accomplished, as his sons gave the king his wine at entertain-

---

[1] *blazed from its ashes.* A metaphor is usually turned into a simile in Latin ; that is to say, a word, 'quasi' or 'velut,' is introduced. Cf. Cic. Epist. iii. 2, 'facilior erit mihi quasi decursus, mei temporis.'

[2] *who had no alternative*, &c. Cf. Cic. Phil. viii. 1, 'quum inter bellum et pacem nihil medium sit.' Turn by 'to whom there was nothing between,' &c.

[3] *who had scarcely heard . . . before.* Cf. Cæs. B. Gall. vi. 7, 'vix agmen novissimum processerat quum,' &c. 'Vix' followed by 'et' seems poetical. Cicero uses 'commodum' in his letters in the same sense. Cf. ad Att. xiii. 9, 'commodum discesseras heri quum Trebatius venit.' Or turn by 'who, the approach of the enemy being

scarcely heard,' &c. (vixdum).

[4] *one or more.* Cf. Cic. pro Mur. xxi., 'neque in uno aut altero animadversum est.'

[5] *To keep any one fully employed.* Cf. Cic. Epist. iii. 10, 'de temeritate eorum qui tibi negotium facesserent.' For 'employed' and 'revolted,' in the next line, the imperfect and pluperfect must be used respectively, because the first action was still going on, the latter was completed.

[6] *this, he affirmed*, &c. No verb in Latin is required to introduce a speech, but the infinitive mood is used, depending on 'dixit,' or a similar word understood. Cf. Tac. Ann. xiv. 8, 'sin facinus patraturus venisset, nihil se de filio credere (*sc.* dixit).'

ments. The letter which the consuls sent to Pyrrhus on this occasion was to this effect : The Roman consuls send health to king Pyrrhus. On account of the injuries received from you, we are ever anxious to oppose you with ardour and with enmity. But for the sake of general example and fidelity, we wish you to be preserved, that we may finally conquer you in arms. Nicias, your familiar friend, come to us, asking of us a reward if he should destroy you privately. To this we refused our assent ; nor might he for this expect any advantage [1] from us ; at the same time we thought proper to inform you of this, lest if any such thing happened, the world might have thought it done by our suggestion ; [2] and because it is not agreeable to us to contend by means of perjury or fraud. Unless you take heed, you will perish.

XXXI.

Once upon a time, a king walking in his garden saw some roses which were yet buds,[3] breathing an ineffable sweetness. He thought, if these shed such sweetness while yet they are buds, what will they do when they are fully blown ?[4]   After a while the king entered the garden anew, thinking to find [5] the roses now blown, and to delight himself with their fragrance ; but on arriving [6] at the place, he found them pale and withered. He exclaimed with regret, " Had I gathered them while yet tender and young, and while they gave forth their sweetness, I might have delighted myself with them ; but now I have no

[1] *expect any advantage.* Cf. Cic. De Senec. xviii., 'fructus capit utilitatis extremos.'

[2] *at our suggestion.* Cf. Liv. xxxvii. 47, 'auctore eo patres consuerunt.'

[3] *roses which were yet buds.* Turn by 'roses scarcely yet opened,' or 'not increased into flowers.'

[4] *To be fully blown.* Use 'in folia exire,' or cf. Virg. Georg. ii. 333, 'Pampinus frondes explicat omnes.'

[5] *thinking to find.* Avoid putting 'credens invenire.' The infinitive present can never be used except to denote time contemporaneous with the governing verb. 'Credens (se) invenire' can only mean 'thinking that he was finding.' 'To find' is here really future compared to 'thinking ;' as in 'hope to come,' 'promise to come,' &c. ; and must be turned by the future infinitive.

[6] *on arriving.* Cf. Cic. Verr. iv. 29, 'postenquam ad causam dicendam ventum est.'

pleasure in them." The next year the king walked in his garden; and finding rose-buds, he commanded his servants, "Gather them, that I may enjoy them before [1] they wither, as last year they did." TRENCH.

XXXII.

But this did not prevent him from being active in public business, frugal in his own : a quality [2] not often found in those princes who are given to pleasure. No one bore labour, cold, and hunger better than he, which is proved by his frequent marches against the rebels in person. [3] He was severe to the nobility, [4] under pretence of favouring the poorer classes, which made them less ready to come forward when his occasion required it.

XXXIII.

He not only undertook nothing against the exiles, but even cautioned and advised Thrasybulus to commit no hostilities [5] against him. It would certainly have been a bold thing to trust a Spartan, but it would have been well [6] if Thrasybulus had on that occasion done so at once. But he did not do so until he had been once defeated by Pausanias. An engagement took place, in which the Lacedæmonians were at first repulsed, and many fell.

---

[1] *before.* 'Prius' and 'quam' are usually separated. Cf. Cic. ad Att. iv. 1, 'Nihil prius mihi faciendum putavi quam ut tibi gratularer.' The same is true of 'post quam,' 'ante quam,' &c.

[2] *a quality not often found.* Avoid 'qualitas,' which is only a philosophical term. Turn by 'id quod,' or 'quæ res.' For '*is not often found*' use 'rarò contigit,' as the quality is a good one, the verb generally being used in a good sense. Cf. Hor. Epist. II. ii. 41, 'mihi Romæ nutriri contigit;' also Cic. Cat. iii. 6, 'quod mihi primum contigit.'

[3] *in person.* Not 'in suâ personâ,' which would rather perhaps

mean 'in his own character.'

[4] *nobility.* 'Nobilitas' is sometimes used in this sense. Cf. Liv. xxvi. 12, 'Nobilitas rem publicam deseruerat.' Cf. Tac. Ann. xii. 20.

[5] *advised to commit no hostilities.* See Introd. III. on the constructions of 'moneo;' and observe that 'ut nihil,' 'ut nemo,' &c. are replaced by 'ne quid,' 'ne quis,' &c. unless the sentence expresses a consequence. 'Alexander edixit *ne quis* alius quàm Apelles pingeret;' 'Apelles ab Alexandro tanti fiebat *ut* à *nullo* alio pingi vellet,' are the two forms.

[6] *it would have been well.* Cf. Cic. Verr. v. 51, 'Intelliget secum pessimè actum esse.'

One would imagine [1] that Pausanias was now provoked, and would have commenced an implacable war ; but he was content with driving the Athenians back, and again admonished them to be quiet. NIEBUHR.

XXXIV.

At Tarentum too the people were not in any hurry [2] about the war, and a party of peace [3] were for negotiating ; since the Romans, notwithstanding their distance, were very dangerous to the Tarentines, for the Romans had been preparing for the war against them for several years, by the establishment of fortified places. But the opinion that Pyrrhus should be invited gained the upper hand. [4] The fact that this plan [5] was adopted without hesitation, can be explained only by the general enthusiasm for Pyrrhus ; for the Athenians too, after having experienced much base treachery, invited him, with his guard, to offer up sacrifices on the Acropolis. Pyrrhus received pressing invitations from the Samnites, Lucanians, and Tarentines ; and we may add without hesitation, that all those nations offered him the supreme command. [6] NIEBUHR.

XXXV.

In the meantime Mummius arrived and took the place [7] of Metellus. He had no such feelings towards the Achæans as his predecessor, [8] who returned to Rome.

---

[1] *One would imagine.* Cf. Tac. Hist. i. 45, 'alium crederes senatum' (or 'credas').

[2] *To be in any hurry*, 'Qd festinantius agere,' or 'nimiam celoritatem adhibere ;' also cf. Cic. Epist. vii. 8, 'quin tu urges istam occasionem et facultatem.'

[3] *a party of peace*, &c. Turn by 'there were some who,' &c.

[4] *An opinion gained the upper hand.* Cf. Liv. ii. 4, 'quum in senatu vicisset sententia,' &c.; or cf. 'suggestum adornari placuit.' (Liv.)

[5] *The fact that this plan*, &c. Turn by 'The zeal for Pyrrhus

caused this plan to be adopted,' or 'the cause of which plan must be sought from (repetere) the zeal,' &c.

[6] *offered him the supreme command.* Cf. Cic. Phil. ii. 34, 'Cæsari Antonium populi jussu regnum detulisse.' For the preceding words cf. Liv. i. 1, 'satis constat in Trojanos sævitum esse.'

[7] *took the place of.* Cf. Ex. VIII. ad fin.

[8] *predecessor.* Avoid 'predecessor ;' turn by 'is cujus in locum suffectus est,' or 'is qui proximus erat,' or a similar phrase.

Mummius now had an army of 23,000 foot and three thousand horse, while the Achæans had only 14,000 foot and a few hundred horse. The Achæans were encamped on the Isthmus in a strong position; but this was of no avail. The Romans had a fleet furnished by their allies, while the Greeks had no ships, and the Roman fleet cruised along the whole coast [1] of Peloponnesus, landing everywhere and ravaging the country with the most fearful cruelty. What Themistocles had said to the Peloponnesians, when they wanted to fortify themselves on the Isthmus, now came to pass; the contingents [2] dispersed in all directions, in order to protect their own towns, without being able to do so. A somewhat favourable engagement,[3] in which they defeated a detachment of the Romans, which had ventured too far and was not duly supported, made the Achæans completely mad; and being thus encouraged, they thoughtlessly attacked the Roman army. But their small advantage was immediately neutralised [4] by a fatal blow; for in a great and decisive battle the Achæans were so completely routed,[5] that they were not even able to throw themselves into Corinth. The cavalry fled immediately; the infantry maintained its ground better; but in the end all fled in different directions to the mountains.   NIEBUHR.

XXXVI.

The Roman army proceeded from Epirus to Thessaly; but being too weak, it could not attack Perseus, nor could it place full confidence in the Greeks in its rear. Its commander, the consul Marcius Philippus, therefore induced Perseus to conclude an armistice, in order to carry

[1] *cruised along the coasts.* Cf. Stat. Theb. v. 472, 'mea littora rectis prætervectus aquis.'

[2] *contingents.* 'Socii,' or 'auxilia.'

[3] *A somewhat favourable engagement.* Turn by 'the Achæans . . . when they had repulsed . . . are so carried away as to attack,' &c. Cf. Cic. ad Att. i. 8, 'Sic studio efferi-

mur ut reprehendendi simus.'

[4] *neutralised,* &c. Turn by 'which victory lest it should be of any use, a fatal disaster prevented;' and cf. Cic. ad Att. i. 1, 'Satrius magno usui fuit.'

[5] *so routed that they were not able.* Cf. Cic. in. Pison. c. xxvi., 'Hoc inferius est quàm ut avo tuo dignum esse videatur.'

on negotiations of peace; and Perseus, though he had been successful in the first engagement, allowed himself to be duped instead of following up his advantages.[1] The Romans, on the other hand, employed this time in stirring up the Greeks and strengthening themselves. The Bœotians being without a Macedonian garrison, regretted their former steps, because the Romans had removed the most zealous partisans of Macedonia, and demanded that those nations which did not stand by Perseus[2] should publicly declare against him. In consequence of this, several tribes abandoned the alliance. NIEBUHR.

XXXVII.

(ST. JOHN'S COLLEGE, 1846.)

The commander also must be of repute,[3] so that the soldiers may be confident of his wisdom: and they shall always be so,[4] when they perceive him to be a man orderly, careful, and courageous, and that maintains well and with esteem the majesty of his dignity; and he shall always be able to do so while he punisheth their faults, while he tires not out the soldiers to no purpose, keeps his word with them, shews them an easy way to vanquish the enemy; those things that may endanger them conceals from them, or if they be evident, by his speeches lessens their opinion[5] of them; which things well observed are a great occasion of confidence[6] in the army. And the Romans used, more-

[1] *instead of following up his advantages.* 'Quum potuisset,' or 'debuisset, victoriâ uti,' or 'nihil a victoriâ cessare.'

[2] *which did not stand by Perseus.* Cf. Liv. xxvi. 41, 'Quum dii prope ipsi cum Hannibale starent.' Cf. also Cic. in Bruto lxxix, 'nemo steterit a senatu et a bonorum causâ.' 'Facere cum qo,' and 'à qo,' is used in the same sense. Cf. Cic. de Invent. i. 48, 'quod nihilo magis ab adversariis quàm à nobis facit.'

[3] *of repute.* Cf. Cic. de Amic.

ii., 'perfectus et spectatus vir.'

[4] *and they shall always be so.* Avoid using 'ita' or 'sic' in such cases; turn by 'id quod semper fiet,' or repeat the verb, 'and they will be confident.'

[5] *lessens their opinion.* Cf. Liv. iii. 21, 'Mirer si vana vestra ad plebem auctoritas est? Vos elevatis cam.'

[6] *occasion of confidence.* Cf. Ter. Heaut. III. ii. 1, 'addere animos alicui;' and Cæs. B. Gall. vii. 70, 'nostris augetur animus.'

over, to make their armies thus confident by way of
religion; from hence proceeded, that by their soothsayings
and auspices they created their consuls, they levied their
soldiers, marched with their armies, and fought their
battles; and without having done some of these things,
never would a good or discreet commander have put anything to hazard,[1] deeming that he might easily lose, unless
his soldiers had first understood that the gods were on
their side. And when any consul or captain of theirs
should have fought contrary to the auspices, they would
have punished him, as they did Claudius Pulcher.

XXXVIII.

Metellus now appeared before Corinth. Animated by
a feeling of humanity, he wished to spare the city: such a
magnificent ancient city was indeed something venerable
to many a Roman, and the idea of destroying it[2] was
terrible to Metellus. It is also possible that he grudged
the consul Mummius, who was already advancing in quick
marches,[3] the honour of bringing the war to a close. Once
more Metellus sent some Greeks to the army, affording,
according to Roman notions.[4] fair terms if they would but
lay down their arms. What else could he have done?
But Diæus, who knew that his life was forfeited,[5] goaded
the poor people to madness. The Achæans, believing that
Metellus had offered peace from a feeling of weakness,
nearly killed the ambassadors, and Diæus did not set them
free until a ransom of 10,000 drachmas was paid. The
hypostrategus,[6] who was favourable to the Romans, was
tortured.   NIEBUHR.

[1] *put anything to hazard.* Cf.
Liv. i. 23, 'in dubiam imperii ser-
vitiique aleam imus.' Cf. also Liv.
xlii. 59, 'dare summam rerum in
aleam,' or 'tentare fortunam belli.'

[2] *the idea of destroying it*, &c.
Turn by 'from destroying which he
was prevented by scruple.' Cf. Cic.
Cat. iii. 6, 'ut quæ religio Mario
non fuerat quominus prætorem
occideret.' Cf. also Ter. Heaut. II.

i. 16, 'hoc facere religio est.'

[3] *quick marches.* Cf. Cæs. B.
Gall. i. 7, 'quam maximis potest
itineribus in Galliam contendit.'

[4] *according to Roman notions.*
Cf. Cic. de Senec. iv., 'multæ etiam
ut in homine Romano litteræ.'

[5] *his life was forfeited.* Use
'pœnam capitis commerere,' or
'de quo actum esse.'

[6] *hypostrategus.* Use 'legatus.

XXXIX.

When the Athenians, in the war with the Lacedæmonians,[1] received many defeats both by sea and land, they sent a message to the oracle of Jupiter Ammon, to ask the reason why they who erected so many temples to the gods, and adorned them with such costly offerings; why they who had instituted so many festivals, and accompanied them with such pomps and ceremonies; in short, why they who had slain so many hecatombs at their altars, should be less successful than the Lacedæmonians, who fell so short of them in these particulars.[2] To this, says he, the oracle made the following reply, "I am better pleased[3] with the prayers of the Lacedæmonians than with all the oblations of the Greeks." SPECTATOR.

XL.

The accusation was then directed[4] against the other generals. Two of them made their escape. Theramenes and Thrasybulus were acquitted, and the remainder were brought to trial and condemned. On that occasion Socrates, who was then a member of the council, was bold enough to speak against so severe a judgment, and exerted himself to save[5] the unfortunate men, but in vain. In order to obtain their acquittal, it was proposed to judge them one by one;[6] but the votes were taken upon them in a body, and all were sentenced at once to drink the hemlock. It was on that occasion that Diomedon, when he was led away into prison to drink the poison, said to the people, "We pardon you: may that which you

---

[1] *the war with the Lacedæmonians,* 'bellum contra Lacedæmonios susceptum;' not simply 'bellum contra Lacedæmonios:' a sentence can seldom be appended to a noun in this way, unless a participle be used.

[2] *fell short of them in these particulars,* 'haudquaquam in hâc' ro sibi pares.'

[3] *I am better pleased.* Turn by the oratio obliqua, 'replied that

it was better pleased,' &c. See Introd. IV.

[4] *the accusation was then directed.* Turn by ' the other generals are accused:' 'insimulare qm,' 'arguere,' 'crimen inferre ci.'

[5] *exerted himself to save.* Cf. Cic. pro Sext. lxvi., 'hæc qui pro virili parte defendunt.'

[6] *to judge them one by one.* Use 'de quoque viritim sententiam ferre.'

have done to us not turn out to your own misfortune! But the vows of gratitude which we have made to the gods you must perform,[1] because we cannot." A noble trait![2] The man who spoke thus did not harbour the desire to take vengeance on his country, as Camillus is said to have done. NIEBUHR.

XLI.

Socrates meeting his pupil Alcibiades as he was going to his devotions,[3] and observing his eyes to be fixed upon the earth[4] with great seriousness and attention, tells him that he had reason[5] to be thoughtful on that occasion, since it was possible for a man to bring down evils upon himself by his own prayers; and that those things which the gods send him in answer to his petitions[6] might turn to his destruction. "This," says he,[7] "may not only happen when a man prays for what he knows is mischievous in its own nature, as Œdipus implored the gods to sow dissension among his sons; but when he prays for what he believes would be for his good, and against[8] what he believes would be to his detriment." SPECTATOR.

XLII.

(ST. JOHN'S COLLEGE, 1845.)

The ancients universally esteemed agriculture to be the proper business for freemen, as well as the proper school[9]

---

[1] the vows . . . you must perform. Cf. Tac. Ann. xv. 23, 'votaque publicè susceperat quæ exsoluta.'

[2] A noble trait! 'O præclara hominis vox!' or 'O rem dictu præclaram!'

[3] going to his devotions. Use 'preces adhibere diis' (Cic. de Nat. Deor. i. 2), or cf. Val. Flac. iv. 547, 'ille ducem nec ferre preces.'

[4] eyes fixed on the earth. Cf. Tac. Hist. iv. 72, 'stabant mœstæ fixis in terram oculis;' also, 'oculos in terram dejicere.'

[5] he had reason to be, &c. Cf. Hor. Epist. II. i. 30, 'non est quod multa loquamur;' or turn by 'non temerè cogitabundum esse.'

[6] in answer to his petitions. Cf. Juv. Sat. x. 6, 'Evertere domos totas optantibus ipsis di faciles.'

[7] This, says he, &c. Omit 'says he,' and use the infinitive of the oratio obliqua. See Introd. IV.

[8] prays against. Cf. Liv. xxxix. 35,. 'Filium mittere Romam ad deprecandam iram senatus statuit.'

[9] the proper school. Cf. Cic. de Fin. i. 13, 'Sapientiâ præceptrice,

for soldiers. The countryman, says Cato, has the fewest
evil thoughts. In him the old stock [1] of the nation is preserved; while it changes in cities where foreign merchants
and tradesmen settle, and the natives remove whither-
soever gain lures them. In every country where slavery
prevails, freedmen seek their livelihood [2] by occupations of
this kind, in which they not unfrequently grow wealthy.
Thus, among the ancients, such trades were mostly in the
hands of this class, and were therefore thought disreputable
to a citizen. Hence the opinion that admitting the artisans
to full civic rights [3] was a hazardous measure.

XLIII.

(Before beginning this Exercise, see Introd. IV.)

It was said by ancient poets that there were islands in
the ocean, to which the souls of those who have lived a
holy and religious life are carried after death; that they
lived there in mutual happiness and pleasure in a most
delightful [4] garden, ever variegated and enamelled [5] with a
glittering variety of flowers most pleasing to sight and
smell; that the sky there always shines, the trees always
bloom, the grass always springs, and all nature smiles;
that gentle breezes blow continually, by which the foliage
of the trees is softly fanned, and soothes the ear with its
rustling. There are there also an innumerable number of
never-dying birds, which, pouring forth their melodious
songs, for ever thrill the senses [6] of those that hear them
with ineffable delight.

in tranquillitate vivi potest.' Or
turn by 'fit to train soldiers,' 'in-
stituere,' or 'informare.' Avoid
'apta :nstituere.' Cf. Cic. de Nat.
Deor. ii. 55, 'quædam raritas et
mollitudo ad hauriendum spiritum
aptissima.'

[1] the old stock. For the usage of
metaphors, see note on Ex. XXIX.

[2] seek their livelihood. Cf.Phædr.
iii. 16, 'solitæ victum in tenebris
quærere.'

[3] To admit to full civic rights.
Cf. Cic. pro Arch. 4, 'ascribi se in
eam civitatem voluit.' Cf. also in

the same place, 'tot annis ante
civitatem datam.' Also, 'in civitatem recipere.'

[4] delightful. Cf. Cic. ad Att.
xvi. 3, 'in prædiolis satis amœnis.'
This adjective is generally used of
places, gardens, &c.; although not
always, for Livy has 'cultus amœ-
nior.'

[5] enamelled, &c. Cf. de Nat.
Deor. ii. 37, 'distinctum et ornatum
cœlum astris.'

[6] thrill the senses. Use 'intimos
sensus permulcere,' or 'mira dul-
cedine afficere.'

XLIV.

These fables and the like are related by poets, as I have said ; respecting those islands traditions differ [1] about their situation, for while most place them, after Homer's example, on the confines of Spain, there are some who say that they are in the neighbourhood of India.　The most strange and absurd account of all which I met with in a Greek grammarian [2] is, that they are in Britain.　He relates the following story : That there are certain men on the shore of that sea which washes the British Isles, who live by fishing,[3] and who are under French government, without, however, being tributaries ; they sometimes, while sleeping in their houses, hear a voice by which they are called, and perceive the presence of a number of men before their doors clapping their hands gaily ; but upon waking and going out of doors, no one is to be seen ;[4] they only find some strange boats, which from the sound they know to be full of sailors.

XLV.

Philopœmen applied the rights belonging to the league in their widest sense,[5] and was determined to reconquer Messenia by force of arms.　He set out against the place with cavalry, probably to relieve [6] Corone ; but he was taken aback [7] by an unfortunate accident, so that he saw no way of escaping ; yet he manœuvred so skilfully, that

---

[1] *traditions differ.*　See Ex. XVIII.　Cf. Liv. xxii. 61, 'mirari adeð discrepare inter auctores queas.'

[2] *in a grammarian.*　When a writer is quoted, without mention of the particular work, 'apud' is used.　Cf. Cic. de Fin. v. 10, 'ut ille apud Terentium,' &c.

[3] *live by fishing.*　Use 'piscibus capiundis victum quærere.'

[4] *is to be seen.*　Not 'videndum esse,' for there is no idea of necessity ; nor 'est videri,' which is an impossible construction ; but the simple infinitive.

[5] *in the widest sense.*　Cf. Cic. pro Mur. xxxi., 'mitiorem in partem interpretarere.'

[6] *probably to relieve.*　Turn by 'ut videbatur obsidione soluturus,' and observe that 'videor' in this sense is used generally personally, not impersonally ; not 'ut videbatur cupidi erant,' for instance, but 'ut videbantur,' &c.

[7] *taken aback*, &c.　Turn by 'being overpowered (oppressus) . . . although there was . . . still by manœuvring skilfully (re bene gestâ),' &c.

he saved the greater part of his troops from the defile ; but he himself was wounded, taken prisoner, and put to death by the Messenians with unpardonable cruelty : he was obliged to drink the hemlock in his seventieth year. But the Messenians too did not commit this act of inhumanity with impunity.[1] The Achæans, commanded by Lycortas, invaded Messenia with a great force, overpowered the enemy, conquered the city, and compelled Messene again to enter the confederacy. The authors of the murder of Philopœmen were punished. Dinocrates made away with himself ;[2] and of his principal accomplices, some were put to death, and others sent into exile. The latter applied to the Romans, who commanded the Achæans to restore the exiles to their country. This demand, indeed, greatly exasperated the Achæans, but under their strategus, Callicrates, they yielded without further remonstrance.

NIEBUHR.

XLVI.

Pausanias relates, in his book on Attica,[3] that the Athenians having been praised by Pindar in a song, valued so highly the compliment of that lofty and sublime poet, that they sent him numerous gifts on that account, and set up his statue in their city. It is not therefore wonderful if,[4] in those days, there were many excellent poets, since those who excelled in that talent were both rewarded with the greatest gifts and the highest honours. In our age, that once harmonious choir of the Muses is reduced to silence, and that avarice which has closed the purses of the wealthy has also dammed up[5] the stream of the water of Helicon.

---

[1] *commit with impunity.* Cf. Ter. Eun. V. ii. 13, 'credin' to impuno abiturum ;' and Tac. Ann. iii. 70, 'neque tantum maleficium impune habendum.'

[2] *made away with himself,* 'mortem sibi inferre,' or 'consciscere.'

[3] *his book on Attica.* Use 'Attica' (neut. plur.); cf. Hellenica, Iroica, &c.; or 'liber de Atticâ

scriptus :' but 'liber de Atticâ, without a participle, is not a usual Latin form. See on Ex. xxxix.

[4] *wonderful if.* 'Mirum si.' with an indicative, as there is nothing doubtful in the 'if.' Of course, if 'si' states a pure hypothesis, it requires the subjunctive.

[5] *dammed up the stream.* Cf. Cæs. B. Civ. iii. 48, 'omnia flumina et rivos operibus obstruxerat.'

But what Pausanias slightly touches on respecting Pindar, Æschines relates more at length in one of his Epistles ; for he says that, having commended the city of Athens, he was fined by his fellow-citizens, who were displeased that he had given such praise to foreigners rather than his own people. When the Athenians knew this, they immediately sent him double the sum [1] which had been exacted as a fine, and honoured him with a brazen statue.

XLVII.

He was a resolute and enterprising man, and personally as a general not contemptible, and very ingenious, but withal he was a robber and a complete monster ; [2] all the horrors which are related of him may be unhesitatingly believed. He seems to have aimed at utterly annihilating the ancient race of the Spartans ; he partly murdered and partly exiled them, and even the exiles were not safe against his hired assassins whom he kept in all the towns. Others he robbed of their property ; he connected the wealthy with his own family ; gave the wives and daughters of the exiles in marriage partly to his mercenaries, and partly to emancipated slaves ; and in this manner he changed Lacedæmon into an asylum for the greatest murderers and criminals. His subjects were regularly plundered by him ; and whenever they were unable to satisfy his demands,[3] he tortured them in the most cruel manner. Nabis was still in possession of Argos, which, as I have already stated, had during the war been surrendered to him by the Macedonian commander. As, however, Argos had been Achæan, a war broke out between him and the Achæans. Flamininus assisted them, being induced to do so by the equivocal conduct [4] of Nabis ; but his real

---

[1] *double the sum which,* &c. Turn by ' double of that money in which he had been mulcted being sent,' &c.

[2] *a complete monster.* Use ' homo monstruosus' (cf. ' vitâ scriptisque monstruosus,' or ' portentosus').

Below, 'to keep assassins' is ' alere sicarios.'

[3] *satisfy his demands.* Use ' postulata facere,' or ' concedere postulationi es ' (Cic. pro Mur. xxiii.).

[4] *equivocal conduct.* Use ' es ambigua ratio agendi.'

object was to obtain the supreme command of the war, in order that the destruction of the tyrant might not be the end of the struggle. NIEBUHR.

XLVIII.

We were riding together to Richmond, in a party, many of whom [1] might be called sensible men. The sky was beautifully clear, and not obscured by a cloud in any part. Of a sudden, the Count, raising his eyes to heaven, exclaimed, " Good heavens ! what do I see ! may a merciful Providence [2] avert this omen." Those who were riding nearest to the Count asked him what he saw, upon which he replied, " Do you not see that enormous dragon, with fiery horns and circling tail ?" [3] As they declared that they could not see it, he begged them to look more attentively ; and pointing with his finger, he showed them the exact spot [4] where the phenomenon might be seen. They still declared themselves unable to see it, till at last one of them, not wishing to be thought unable [5] to see it, declared that he saw it too ; one after another followed his example ; and at length the strange appearance was declared to be distinctly visible to all. Within three days the story was noised abroad throughout England, and there was no lack of inquiries into the design of so strange an appearance [6] in the heavens.

XLIX.

" We must therefore wait until such time as we may learn how we ought to behave [7] ourselves towards the gods and towards men." " But when will that time come," says Alcibiades, " and who is it that will instruct us ? for I

[1] *many of whom*, &c. Turn by ' homines, ut videbamur, non insulsi,' or similar phrase.

[2] *may a merciful Providence*, &c. Cf. Cic. ad Att. ix. 2, ' dii inquis averruncent.' Also ' hæc à nobis averruncetur dementia.'

[3] *circling tail*, ' cauda in orbem sinuata.'

[4] *exact spot where*, &c. Turn by ' locum ipsum miraculi.'

[5] *thought unable to see*, &c. Cf. Cic. Tusc. v. 40, ' oculis et auribus captus.'

[6] *design of so strange an appearance*. Use some phrase like ' qd sibi voluit istud prodigium.'

[7] *how we ought to behave*. Use ' qualem esse,' or ' qualem se præbere oportet.'

would fain see this man, whoever he is." "It is one," says
Socrates, "who takes care of you ; but as Homer tells us
that Minerva removed the mist from Diomede's eyes, that
he might plainly discover both gods and men, so the darkness that hangs upon your mind must be removed before
you are able to discern what is good and what is evil."
"Let him remove from my mind," says Alcibiades, "the
darkness and what else he pleases ; I am determined[1] to
refuse nothing he shall order me, whoever he is, so that I
may become the better man by it."   SPECTATOR.

(Turn the whole extract, for practice, by the oratio obliqua.)

L.

During the minority[2] of the latter, the Romans treated
him with unexampled injustice. They first took from him
Phrygia, because their attention had been directed to the
importance of that state. This he never forgot. But they
also endeavoured to injure him otherwise in every possible
way, and to limit his powers more and more. Under these
circumstances he grew up thirsting for revenge.[3] During
the Cimbrian war, the Romans had no time to keep their
eyes on him. He was a man of great mind, and having
now grown up to the age of manhood,[4] he formed a profound
plan of revenge. He first tried to strengthen his kingdom.
Thus he carried on wars on the Bosphorus as far as the
Borysthenes, and there subdued all the nations as far as
the Don. His general, Neoptolemus, built fortresses there.
His whole plan was directed against Rome ; and had he been
a contemporary of Hannibal, it is very probable that Rome
would have been crushed. If he had only had another
people than Asiatics, the destruction of Rome would have
been possible. All his designs were excellent, but all
failed in their execution,[5] on account of the miserable

[1] *I am determined.* Cf. Cic. de
Or. ii. 33, 'quum diceret sibi certum esse a judiciis discedere.'

[2] *During the minority,* &c. Cf.
Senec. Ep. 33, 'isti qui nunquam
tutelæ suæ fiunt.'

[3] *thirsting for revenge.* Cf. Tac.

Ann. iv. 25, 'se quisque ultione
et sanguine explebant. Cf. also
Cic. ad Q. Frat. iii. 5, 'nec sitio
honores nec desidero gloriam.'

[4] *grown up to manhood.* Cf.
'quum se jam corroboravisset.'

[5] *failed in execution.* Cf. **Liv.**

character of his subjects. His plan, even at an early period, was to throw the Bastarnæ[1] and Getæ from Dacia upon Italy, while he himself was to attack the Romans in Asia, and expel them from those countries.

NIEBUHR.

LI.

The putting of oaths[2] often makes men more active in observing their agreements ; for though it be the part of a good man to keep faith without any such obligation, nevertheless we do find it happen[3] that such as it likes not to fulfil what they have taken in hand find some excuse ; whereas none but a godless fellow shall do so in a matter whereto God is his witness. Wisely therefore, and cunningly, does Medea in Euripides withhold instant belief[4] in Ægeus when he promised her a safe asylum, asking him to confirm his promise by an oath ; and when in surprise he asked her[5] if she did not believe him, the cunning and shrewd lady is represented to have answered . . . . which verses, as commonly read, are corrupt in several places, and are not methinks understood by the scholiast. I do thus therefore interpret them : " I do trust you ; but the house of Pelias is hostile to me, and so is Creon. To Pelias and Creon, if they come to take me from your confines, you will not permit it, and will not give me up to them, if you promise me on oath."

LII.

What reason can be assigned for the fact, that while the wishes of every individual are by the very guidance and impulse of nature directed towards what is good, so

xxviii. 31, 'spem ad irritum redactam ;' also ' in irritum revolvi ' (Tac. Hist. iii. 26), or ' cadere ' (Hist. iii. 53).

[1] *to throw the Bastarnæ,* &c. Cf. Sil. xvii. 353, ' juvenemque ferocem immisisti Latio.'

[2] *The putting of oaths.* Use ' jusjurandum interpositum,' or

' interposita jurisjurandi religio.'

[3] *we find it happen.* Cf. Liv. xxvi. 23, ' forte ita incidit ut comitiis nunciaretur.'

[4] *withhold instant belief.* Turn by a participle, making 'asking' the main verb, and use ' fide derogatâ.'

[5] *asked if.* See Ex. XXVII.

small a portion of mankind attain to what is really such ? That such is the case is evident : for this desire of good is plainly natural : now that which is natural must exist in the whole race : it follows then that none, however perverted his mind, can fail to direct his every design and project to that which is good, or which he considers to be so. Now there are four things which I would notice[1] as the causes by which most men are prevented from the attainment of what is really great and good. In some it is error of judgment, and that in two ways : either they are shackled by false views, and so, passing over what is really good, they embrace some delusive and profitless object ; or having decided truly enough what ought to be the object of their pursuit, they set about attaining it in other ways but the right.[2] In another class it is a want of perseverance and constancy : having at first set themselves to what is good, and entered on the path which leads to their object, they afterwards take another direction, either frightened by the difficulties which arise, or drawn aside by their own levity, and so either resign themselves to inactivity, or at any rate leave off the urgent pursuit[3] of that which they had originally set before them. Others, lastly, though they form a true judgment, and persevere in the plan they have laid down, are hindered by the deficiency of their powers from attaining that which they desire.

LIII.

Pyrrhus, who wished to defer a decisive battle[4] till he was joined by his allies, wrote to the consul, demanding to be accepted as arbitrator between the Romans and Tarentines. Lævinus answered, that the king himself must first make amends[5] for having invaded Italy, and

---

[1] *I would notice.* Use the perfect subjunctive in such phrases. Cf. Tac. Germ. ii., 'ipsos Germanos crediderim mixtos.'

[2] *other ways but the right.* Use 'aliis quam quibus decet (quærere) incipiunt quærere viis.' Observe not to omit the relative.

[3] *leave off the urgent pursuit,* &c. Cf. Hor. Sat. II. vii. 6, 'urget propositum.'

[4] *a decisive battle.* See Ex. XI.

[5] *make amends.* Cf. Cæs. B. G. v. 1, 'se paratos esse demonstrant de injuriis satisfacere.'

that war must decide between them. The hostile armies met on the banks of the Siris, where the consul was compelled, by fear of scarcity among his troops, to force a battle. The Romans fought like lions;[1] but the cavalry of Pyrrhus and his elephants, the formidable aspect of which terrified the Romans, decided the day: [2] the Romans took to flight, and perhaps not one of them would have escaped, had not a wounded elephant in his fury turned against his own men and stopped their pursuit. Pyrrhus took the enemy's camp without resistance: he had indeed gained a complete victory. On the following day he visited the field of battle, and seeing the bodies of the Romans, all of whom had fallen with their faces towards the enemy, he exclaimed, "With such soldiers the world were mine; and it would belong to the Romans if I were their commander." But the best part of his own [3] men had fallen; and to those who congratulated him on victory, he replied, "One more such victory, and I shall be obliged to return to Epirus without a single soldier."

SCHMITZ.

LIV.

Perseus from the beginning made preparations against the Romans; he commenced negotiations with Prusias and Antiochus, nay even with Eumenes, and endeavoured to gain popularity [4] among the Greeks. At Athens and in Achaia all intercourse with Macedonia was forbidden even in time of peace; hence all runaway slaves fled to the Macedonians, because the latter, in return, did not allow the Athenians [5] and Achæans to enter their country. But Perseus ordered the runaway slaves to be collected, and

---

[1] *fought like lions.* Use 'acerrime pugnare:' the metaphor does not seem a Latin one.

[2] *decided the day.* Cf. Liv. xxv. 41, 'primus clamor atque impetus rem decrevit.'

[3] *the best part of his own men.* Cf. Tac. Hist. iv. 33, 'Cæsorum in nostris partibus major numerus et imbellior, e Germanis ipsa robora.' Turn the last part of the sentence

by the oratio obliqua: 'replied that, having obtained . . . he must return.'

[4] *gain popularity.* See Ex. XI.

[5] *did not allow the Athenians,&c.* Cf. Cic. pro Rosc. Amer. xxxviii., 'hisce omnes aditus ad Sullam intercludere.' Also, with a varied construction, cf. Cæs. B. G. iii. 23, 'nostros commeatibus intercludere instituunt.'

sent them back to the Achæans, with the request that they should become his friends. The leading men were glad of this opportunity of making peace, without any intention [1] of making the Romans their enemies on that account; but Callicrates, a traitor, deserving to be branded [2] for ever, in order to flatter the Romans in every way, opposed the plan in the assembly, and represented this alliance [3] with Perseus as an act of treachery against Rome, so that an embassy was indeed sent to the king, but his offer was declined. In other states he was more successful : the Bœotians, being favourable to Macedonia, thoughtlessly concluded a treaty with him. Perseus himself, accompanied by a considerable detachment of troops, went to Delphi, offered up sacrifices, and treated the Greeks in a friendly manner; but without doing anything further returned to Macedonia.　　　　　　　　NIEBUHR.

LV.

(Classical Tripos, 1846.)

It seems to me a strange and a thing much to be marveiled, that the laborer, to repose himself, hasteneth, as it were, the course of the sun; that the mariner rowes with all force to attain the port, and with a joyfull crie salutes the descried land; that the traveller is never contented nor quiet till he be at the end of his voyage; and that we, in the meanwhile, tied in this world to a perpetual taske, tossed with continual tempest, tyred with a rough and combersome way, yet cannot see the end of our labour but with grief, nor behold our port but with tears, nor approach our home and quiet abode but with horrour and trembling. This life is but a Penelope's web, wherein we are always doing and undoing; [4] a sea open to all winds; a weary journey thro' extreme heats and colds, over high mountains, steep rocks, and thievish deserts; [5]

[1] *without any intention.* Use 'neque tamen ita ut . . .'

[2] *deserving to be branded.* Cf. Liv. iii. 58, 'ne Claudiæ genti eam inustam maculam vellent,' &c.

[3] *represented this alliance.* Turn by 'fœdus jungere . . . ingratorum esse coarguit.'

[4] *wherein we are doing and undoing,* &c. Use 'telam modò textam semper retexere.'

[5] *thievish deserts.* Cf. Vellej. ii. 73, 'latrociniis ac prædationibus infestato mari,' Cicero has 'via incursionibus infesta.'

and so we terme it in weaving at this web, in rowing at this oar, in passing this miserable way.

LVI.

Yet loe, when death comes to end our worke, when she stretcheth out her armes to pull us into the port, when after so many dangerous passages she would conduct us to our true home and resting-place, instead of[1] rejoycing at the end of our labour, of taking comfort at the sight of our land, of singing at the approach of our happy mansion, we would faine retake our worke in hand, we would again hoise sail to the wind, and willingley undertake our journey anew. We fear more the cure than the disease, the surgeon than the paine, more feeling of death, the end of our miseries,[2] than the endlesse miserie of our life ; we fear that we ought to hope for, and wish that we ought to fear.

LVII.

Antiochus had even before negotiated for peace, and, to speak the truth,[3] had expected nothing[4] but a defeat, in order to be able to accept the terms of the Romans, and to submit to a disgraceful peace without being ashamed of himself. The terms were extremely humiliating : he was obliged to deliver up his ships of war, with the exception of a few, to promise not to keep any elephants for the purposes of war, to cede to the Romans all his possessions in Western Asia, except Cilicia, to pay a war-contribution of 10,000 talents by instalments,[5] and to give Antiochus, his son and heir, as a hostage that he would keep the peace. NIEBUHR.

[1] *instead of,* &c. Avoid 'loco,' or 'in loco gaudendi :' turn by 'quum debeamus.' In long enumerations, endeavour to vary the construction, in Latin, to avoid heaviness.

[2] *end of our miseries than the endless,* &c. Use 'terminum miseriarum quam interminatam miseriam,' &c.

[3] *and to speak the truth.* Not 'dicere verum,' for the infinitive can never be used in this absolute way: use 'ut vera dicam,' or 'dixerim.'

[4] *had expected nothing but a defeat,* &c. Turn by 'apparently (ut videbatur) expected nothing but a defeat, if, accepting . . . he did not blush to . . .' Cf. Cic. de Leg. i. 19, 'pudici erubescunt etiam loqui de pudicitiâ.'

[5] *to pay by instalments.* Cf. Liv. xxxiii. 30, 'mille talentum daret : dimidium præsens, dimidium pensionibus decem annorum.'

LVIII.

At this time Hannibal, a fugitive from his own country, arrived at the court of Antiochus. After the peace, being as great in the administration [1] as he was in the field, he had restored order,[2] especially in the financial department of Carthage, so that the city might one day again be in a condition to resume the war with Rome. For this reason the Romans, after the peace with Philip, contrived to effect his expulsion, and hunted him wherever he was. He fled from Africa to Antiochus, whose court was the only one that was free from Roman influence, and he was at first received in a most honourable manner. This favour, however, ceased very soon; for Antiochus found in him no flatterer,[3] and Hannibal forming a correct estimate.[4] of the king's power, told him the truth about the perverseness of his measures.

LIX.

He made no secret in telling him, that if under the present circumstances he would undertake a war against the Romans, he would run into his own ruin. He was the only one that spoke thus; and some miserable creatures [5] at the court of Antiochus very soon persuaded the king that Hannibal was a traitor and a partisan of the Romans, because he did not sufficiently value the power of the king. While Hannibal dissuaded him from the war, the Ætolians, full of impatience, and with a senselessness [6] which we often find among Greeks, urged him to come over to Europe as soon as possible and commence

[1] *great in the administration,* &c. Cf. Cic. Tusc. v. 19, 'quorum virtus domi militiæque cognita fuerat.'
[2] *restored order,* &c. Use 'vectigalia ordinare.'
[3] *found in him no flatterer.* Turn by 'Hannibal, not flattering Antiochus . . . told him.'
[4] *forming a correct estimate.* Use

'æquam et parem æstimationem facere.'
[5] *some miserable creatures,* 'ex aulicis deterrimi.'
[6] *with a senselessness,* &c. Cf. Cic. pro Domo, xxxii., 'pater si viveret, quâ fuit severitate;' and also Ovid ex Pont. II. ii. 21, 'quæ tua est pietas.'

the war. Antiochus had more faith in them than in the warnings of the great Hannibal, and accelerated the war instead [1] of delaying it. NIEBUHR.

LX.

It is, I admit, a great thing to know the origin and causes of natural phenomena: [2] it is glorious to attain by science unto a comprehension of the positions, size, and relative distances of the stars and of the other heavenly bodies, and above all, to know their influence [3] on this lower world, and to be able to foretell with certainty their operations for ever so many years: [4] this, I had well-nigh said, is worthy of a God. But assuredly it will not be denied, even by the professors [5] of that branch of learning that the knowledge of those matters wherein our diligence is exercised, is more fruitful, and ignorance more injurious. Therefore, while, on the one hand, in power of intellect, and extent of learning, and in marvellousness of subject, we willingly give place to those who treat of points so dark and abstruse; so, on the other hand, they themselves must needs in all fairness acknowledge that our discussions are more necessary, and bring forth more abundant fruit [6] for mankind; for no one has ever been thought less a useful citizen because he did not make himself master of those studies, or even utterly neglected them; while ignorance of these hath not only ruined individuals, but hath damaged and overthrown entire states.

LXI.

Demosthenes went into exile, first, perhaps, to Megara, and afterwards to Ægina. Here we have an anecdote; [7]

[1] *instead of.* Cf. 'adeo non tenuit iram ut palàm diceret.' or 'tantum abfuit ut terror cohiberet ut violentior potestas esset;' or use 'bellum maturare quàm differre malle.'

[2] *natural phenomena.* Use 'res naturales.'

[3] *to know their influence.* Cf. Cic. de Fin. i. 17, 'plus ad vitam miseram adferro momenti.'

[4] *for ever so many years.* Use

'in plures annos.'

[5] *by the professors.* Observe that when the agent is a person, and not a thing, the preposition 'a' or 'ab' must be used; although in later writers this rule is sometimes violated.

[6] *bring forth abundant fruit.* Use 'fructus uberes reddere,' or cf. Cic. 'Asia multos annos fructus vobis non tulit.'

[7] *Here we have an anecdote.*

for on quitting the city he is reported to have said, " O Athens, what three monsters dost thou love ! the owl, the snake, and the people ! and if I had to begin my life afresh, and stood at a point where one road leads to the government of the state and the other to misery, I would choose the latter." Scaliger in his old age expressed a similar sentiment. This story is made use [1] of against Athens ; but all such anecdotes are worthless. However, even if he had uttered such a word in the bitterness of his grief, it would neither be an evidence against him nor against his country. The Athenians had no privilege of being free [2] from faults, any more than other mortals. The same public which at one time raises a man up to the skies, is at another time inclined to condemn him, if fortune turns from him. This fickleness occurs everywhere in the mass of a people ; there is unfortunately in them an inclination to ingratitude : very noble minds alone are free from it.   NIEBUHR.

LXII.

A dervise [3] travelling through Tartary, being arrived [4] at the town of Balk, went into the king's palace by mistake, as thinking it to be a public inn or caravansary.[5] Having looked about him for some time, he entered into a long gallery, where he laid down his wallet, and spread his carpet, in order to repose himself upon it, after the manner of [6] the eastern nations. He had not been long in this

Turn by ' cujus ex urbe proficiscentis scitum illud dictum traditur,' and proceed with the oratio obliqua.

[1] *This story is made use of.* Cf. Cic. Epist. vii. 6, ' Ne sibi vitio verterent quod a patriâ abesset ;' or ' vitio dare.'

[2] *privilege of being free.* Use ' contigit vitiis vacare,' or ' tam Atheniensium quam cæterorum errare fuit.'

[3] *A dervise.* Use ' sacerdos.'

[4] *being arrived.* The passive of ' venio,' like that of ' eo,' is used

impersonally. Cf. Cic. in Verr. iv. 29, ' posteàquam ad causam dicendam ventum est,' and Tac. Ann. xvi. 27, ' e longinquis provinciis veniri.' This is, of course, the only way in which these verbs can be used passively.

[5] *caravansary.* Use ' deversorium.'

[6] *after the manner of.* Cf. Liv. ii. 9, ' ne Orientem morem pellendi reges inultum sineret ;' and Cic. ad Att. x. 7, ' Pompeius Sullano more vincet.'

posture before he was discovered by some of the guards who asked him what was his business in that place. The dervise told them he intended to take up his night's lodging [1] in that caravansary. The guards let him know, in a very angry manner, that the house he was in was not a caravansary, but the king's palace. It happened that the king himself passed through the gallery during this debate, and smiling at the mistake of the dervise, asked him how he could possibly be so dull as not to distinguish a palace from a caravansary. SPECTATOR.

XIII.

The total defeat of the Scottish army, lately mentioned, succeeded this; and when those noble persons within Colchester were advertised of both, they knew [2] well that there was no possibility of relief; nor could they subsist [3] longer, to expect it, being pressed with want of all kind of victual, and having eaten near all their horses. They sent, therefore, to Fairfax to treat about the delivery of the town on reasonable conditions; but he refused to treat or give any conditions, if they would not render to mercy [4] all the officers and gentlemen: the common soldiers [5] he was contented to dismiss. A day or two was spent in deliberating. They within proposed to make a brisk sally, and thereby to shift for themselves as many as could; but they had too few horses, and the few that were left uneaten were too weak for that enterprise.

[1] *take up his night's lodging.* Cf. Cic. Tusc. ii. 17, 'pernoctant venatores in nive.'

[2] *they knew there was,* &c. Cf. Liv. xxxviii. 15, for the phrase, 'obsidione eximere,' or 'liberare,' or 'obsidionem solvere;' or turn by 'they began to despair of external help.'

[3] *nor could they subsist,* &c. Turn by 'nor did victuals suffice to them expecting;' and cf. Cæs. B. Gall. i

16, 'ne pabuli quidem satis magna copia suppetebat.'

[4] *render to mercy.* Use 'hostibus se prout volunt tractandum dedere;' or perhaps cf. Plaut. Amph. I. i. 105, 'deduntque se in ditionem atque in arbitratum Thebano populo.'

[5] *common soldiers.* Cf. Tac. Hist. v. 1, 'Titus plerumque gregario militi mixtus.'

LXIV.

From this period all the Roman writers, whether poets or historians,[1] seem to vie with each other[2] in celebrating the praises of Cicero, as the most illustrious of all their patriots, and the parent of the Roman wit and eloquence, who had done more honour to his country by his writings than all their conquerors by their arms, and extended the bounds of his learning beyond those of their empire ; so that their very emperors, near three centuries after his death, began to reverence him in the class of their inferior deities ;[3] a rank which[4] he would have preserved to this day if he had happened to live in papal Rome,[5] where he could not have failed, from the innocence of his life, of obtaining the honour and title of a saint.[6]

MIDDLETON.

LXV.

" There is not an instance,"[7] says Cicero, " of a man's exerting himself ever with praise and virtue in the dangers of his country, who was not drawn to it by the hopes of glory and a regard to posterity." " Give me a boy," says Quinctilian, " whom praise excites, whom glory warms ;" for such a scholar was sure to answer all his hopes,[8] and do credit to his discipline. " Whether posterity will have any respect[9] for me," says Pliny, " I know not ; but am

[1] *historians.* Rather 'rerum gestarum scriptores,' than 'historici,' which latter word rather seems to be used for persons acquainted with history : although Cicero has 'oratores, philosophi, poetæ, historici.'

[2] *vie with each other.* Cf. Liv. i. 40, ' certatim alter alteri obstrepere ;' also cf. Virg. ii. 64, ' certantque illudere capto.'

[3] *inferior deities.* Cf. the usual phrases, 'sub Divo Julio,' &c.

[4] *a rank which.* Avoid 'gradus qui ;' for this leaves 'gradus' without any possible construction. Use 'quem gradum.'

[5] *papal Rome.* 'Romani qui hodiè sunt.'

[6] *honour and title of a saint.* Use 'ad numerum sanctorum ascribi,' or 'sanctis ascribi,' after Cic. ad Q. F. i. 1, 'hunc ad tuum numerum ascribito.'

[7] *There is not an instance,* &c. Turn by the oratio obliqua, 'Cicero narravit vix quenquam . . . . quin duceretur.'

[8] *answer his hopes.* Cf. Cic. Epist. ii. 5, ' tua virtus opinioni hominum respondet.'

[9] *have any respect for me.* Cf. Tac. Hist. i. 50, ' quibus aliqua cura reipublicæ.'

sure that I have deserved some from it : I will not say
by my wit, for that would be arrogant, but by the zeal,
by the pains, by the reverence which I have always paid
to it."   MIDDLETON's *Cicero.*

LXVI.

I have great hopes, [1] O my judges, that it is infinitely to
my advantage that I am sent to death.   For it must of
necessity be that one of these two things must be the consequence : death must take away all these senses, or convey
me to another life.   If all sense is to be taken away, and
death is no more than that profound sleep without dreams
in which we are sometimes buried, O heavens,[2] how desirable is it to die !   How many days do we know in life
preferable to such a state ?   But if it be true that death is
but a passage to places which they who lived before us do
now inhabit, how much still happier is it to go from those
who call themselves judges, to appear before those that
are really such, and to meet men who have lived with
justice and truth !   Do you think it nothing [3] to speak with
Orpheus, Musæus, Homer, and Hesiod ?   I would indeed
suffer many deaths to enjoy these things.

LXVII.

With what particular delight should I talk to Pala-
medes, Ajax, and others, who, like me, have suffered by
the iniquity of their judges !   I should examine the wisdom of that great prince who carried such mighty forces
against Troy, and argue with Sisyphus upon difficult
points, as I have in conversation here, without being in
danger [4] of being condemned.   But let not those among you
who have pronounced me an innocent man be afraid of
death.   No harm can arrive at a good man whether dead

---

[1] *I have great hopes,* 'Magnâ spe
teneor,' or ' me spes magna tenet.'
[2] *O heavens !* Use ' Di immor-
tales,' or ' Di boni ;' not ' cœlum.'
[3] *Do you think it nothing.* Cf.
Cic. ad Att. xiv. 9, ' quam ista pro
nihilo sunt.' Also ' nihili æstimare,'

' pro nihilo ducere.'
[4] *without being in danger.* Perhaps ' non capito periclitaturus
(Mart. vi. 26), or ' ne capitis dam-
narer non sollicitus,' or ' nullo sup-
plicii metu turbatus,' or perhaps
' damnationis securus.'

or living ; his affairs are under the direction of the gods.
Nor will I believe the fate which is allotted to myself this
day to have arrived by chance ; nor have I aught to say [1]
against my judges or accusers, but that they thought they
did me an injury.   But I detain you too long ; it is time
that I retire to death, and you to your affairs of life :
which of us has the better is known to the gods, but to no
mortal man.   SPECTATOR.

LXVIII.

True glory, then, according to his own definition [2] of it,
is a wide and illustrious fame of many and great benefits
conferred upon our friends, our country, or the whole race
of mankind.   It is not, he says,[3] the empty blast of popular favour, or the applause of the giddy multitude, which
all wise men had ever despised, and none more than himself,—but the consenting praise of all honest men, and the
incorrupt testimony of those who can judge of excellent
merit, which resounds always to virtue, as the echo to the
voice ; and since it is a general companion of good actions,
ought not to be rejected by good men.   That those who
aspire to this glory were not to expect ease, or pleasure,
or tranquillity of life for their pains ; but must expose
themselves to storms and dangers for the public good,
sustain many battles with the audacious and the wicked,
and some even with the powerful ; in short, must behave
themselves so as to give their citizens cause [4] to rejoice that
they had ever been born.   MIDDLETON.

LXIX.

The entire defeat of Anthony's army made all people
presently imagine that the war was at an end, and the
liberty of Rome established : [5] which would probably have

[1] *nor have I aught to say
against.* Use the corresponding
form in Latin, ' non habeo quod
succenseam.'

[2] *according to his own definition.*
Use ' ut ipsius verbis utar.'

[3] *It is not, he says.* Omit ' he
says,' and use the infinitive at
once, and see Introd. IV.; and for

the next words, cf. Hor. III. ii. 20,
' arbitrio popularis auræ.'

[4] *give the citizens cause,* &c. Turn
by ' ut civibus sit quod lætentur
natos esse.'

[5] *the liberty of Rome established.*
Cf. Cic. Epist. ii. 5, ' qui sit rempublicam in veterem libertatem
vindicaturus.'

been the case, if Anthony had either perished in the action or the consuls survived it ; but the death of the consuls, though not felt so sensibly [1] at first, in the midst of their joy for the victory, gave the fatal blow to all Cicero's schemes, and was the immediate cause of the ruin of the Republic. Hirtius was a man of letters and politeness : intimately intrusted with Cæsar's counsels, and employed to write his acts ; but as he was the proper creature of Cæsar,[2] and strongly infected with party, so his views were all bent on supporting the power that had raised him, and serving his patron,[3] not the public. In the beginning therefore of the civil war, when he was Tribune of the people, he published a law, to exclude all, who were in arms with Pompey, from any employment or office in the state ; which made him particularly obnoxious to the Pompeians, who considered him as their most inveterate enemy.

MIDDLETON'S Cicero, Sect. 9.

LXX.

(SIDNEY SUSSEX, 1831.)

Titus, after entering the ruins of the city, and admiring the impregnable strength of the towers, declared that he indeed was the leader of the army, but God was the author of the victory. He commanded his soldiers, wearied with slaughter, to cease from carnage, except where any still chanced to resist : that the leaders, concealed in the subterraneous passages,[4] should be sought after ; that the youths distinguished by their beauty and stature should be reserved for his triumph ; that the more advanced in years be sent into Egypt to the mines. A vast number also were selected to perish in the theatres by the sword and wild beasts : all under seventeen were sold by auction. It

---

[1] *not felt so sensibly.* Turn by 'appearing not so to be regretted by those rejoicing,' &c.

[2] *creature of Cæsar.* Use 'Cæsari deditus.'

[3] *patron.* 'Patronus' hardly seems to be used except in its technical sense, unless in such phrases as 'patronus justitiæ,' &c.

[4] *subterraneous passages.* Cf. Tac. Hist. v. 12, 'cavati sub terrâ montes ;' or Suet. in Cal. lviii., 'quum in cryptâ, per quam transeundum erat.'

is a current report[1] among the Jews, that in this siege 97,000 men were taken prisoners; that 1,100,000[2] fell. Nothing remained of the city except three towers, left as a memorial of victory; at the same time part of the western wall was preserved, to which a garrison was assigned; and Terentius Rufus was appointed governor. Everything else was overturned and polluted by the plough.

LXXI.

We are told there once existed a city where it was a rule[3] to elect some foreigner to the throne when vacant, and then when the newly-elected king was living in security and ease, indulging in pleasure and gaiety, as deeming his sovereignty would continue until death, all at once they would strip[4] off from him his royal dress, and banish him to a far-distant island; and there, destitute of either food or clothing, he was a prey to cold and hunger.[5] It so happened, however, that a man of great natural shrewdness was, in the course of events, raised to the throne. He, unlike his careless predecessors, anxiously set about devising the best schemes he could for his establishment; and on discovering the peculiar custom of the country, and the locality of the island whither the deposed monarchs were banished, he entrusted sums of gold and silver to some faithful slaves, and had them conveyed[6] to the island. At the close of the year[7] an insurrection broke out, and, like his predecessors, he was banished; but while his companions in flight suffered the pangs of hunger, he was enabled to live in plenty.

---

[1] *It is a current report.* Cf. Cic. Verr. ii. 1, 'opinio apud exteras gentes sermone percrebuit.'

[2] *eleven hundred thousand.* Cf. Cæs. B. Gall. v. 13, 'omnis insula est in circuitu vicies centena millia passuum.'

[3] *it was a rule.* Use 'moris erat' (Tac. Hist. i. 15), or 'usitatum est.'

[4] *they would strip.* This 'would' is not, of course, the sign of the subjunctive mood; only an idiom for the imperfect indicative.

[5] *a prey to hunger.* Use 'fame enecari,' or 'excruciari.'

[6] *had them conveyed.* Cf. Cic. ad Att. viii. 5, 'Fasciculum velim cures ad eum perferendum.'

[7] *At the close of the year.* Use 'anno exeunte,' 'extremo anno,' 'extremo anni,' 'exitu' or 'fine anni;' the last four are in Tacitus.

LXXII.

As usual, I have kept you to the last, meaning to write to you a very long letter,[1] and to say to you whatever I had left unsaid, and to say over again whatever I had said to them. And now I am so weary and exhausted, that it is a wonder to me how much of these fine purposes[2] I shall execute. I must tell you, because I have yet told nobody, how much his dispatch of yesterday is admired[3] and approved, as well as the conduct it describes ; nothing could be more able and judicious. With regard to public affairs, we cannot and must not disguise our situation from ourselves. If peace is to be had,[4] we must have it ; war is out of the question ; we have not the means ;[5] what is of all means the most important, the mind ! If we are not at peace, we shall be at nothing : it will be a *rixa* between us and our enemies ; a pulsation[6] on their side, a vapulation on ours. CANNING.

LXXIII.

I ought to tell you something of what has been passing here since you left us. There is but one event, and that is an event for the world. Burke is dead ; how and when the newspapers[7] will tell you. I know the details only from them. But it grows very late,[8] and I very tired,

---

[1] *To write a letter.* Use 'Dare litteras ad qm :' 'dare ei' is to give a letter to any one to carry. Cf. Cic. ad Att. xi. 25, 'quum habebis cui des, et dum erit ad quem des.'

[2] *how much of these fine purposes.* Use 'quantulum ex his quæ magnificè profitear ;' and observe that the real future subjunctive is formed by the future participle and the verb 'sum.'

[3] *is admired*, &c. Turn the sentence actively, as 'admiror' cannot be used passively.

[4] *If peace is to be had.* Avoid the participle in 'dus' here, as there is no idea of necessity, only of possibility ; and cf. Liv. iv. 18, 'frementibus ni copia pugnæ fiat.'

Observe also that 'potest' cannot be used impersonally with an active verb : 'non potest habere' will not do for 'it is not possible to have.'

[5] *we have not the means*, &c., 'deest quo bellum geramus.'

[6] *a pulsation*, &c. Cf. Juv. iii. 289, 'Si rixa est ubi tu pulsas, ego vapulo tantum.'

[7] *newspapers.* Cf. Suet. in Tib. v., 'sic enim in fastos actaque publica relatum est.' For 'details' use 'res singulæ,' or 'τὰ κατὰ μέρος.' Cf. Cic. ad Att. xiii. 22.

[8] *But it grows late*, &c. Turn by 'multâ jam nocte multo labore delassatus sum,' in order to retain something like the repetition of the 'grows.'

though I have yet much to say, having, in truth, said nothing. Now for a very few questions, and I have done. What is your private life and conversation? for I have heard nothing of it from any body. Why does not Morpeth write, as well as the rest of you, in the dispatches? Is he idle? or is it chance? or does he do something else for you that does not appear?[1]   And now, good night.

CANNING.

LXXIV.

But these thirty, having so great power in their hands, were more careful[2] to hold it than to deserve it by faithful execution of that which was committed to them. Therefore they condemned to death such troublesome fellows as were odious to the city, though not punishable therefore by law; which proceeding was by all men highly approved, who considered their lewd condition, but did not withal bethink themselves how easy a thing it would be unto these thirty to take away the lives of innocents by calling them disturbers of the peace, or what else they listed, when condemnation[3] without trial and proof had been once allowed. Having thus plausibly entered into a wicked course of government, they thought it best to fortify themselves with a sure guard ere they broke out[4] into those disorders which they must needs commit for the establishment of their authority.

LXXV.

(CLASSICAL TRIPOS, 1847.)

In the first place, let them consider well what are the characters[5] which they bear among their enemies. Our friends very often flatter us as much as our own hearts.

[1] *that does not appear.* Cf. Cic. de Off. i. 35, 'figuram in quâ esset species honesta posuit in promptu.'

[2] *were more careful,* &c. Cf. Nep. in Dion. c. vi., 'invidiam non lenire obsequio studuit;' and also cf. Ter. Heaut. II. iv. 1, 'studuisti ut formæ mores consimiles forent.'

[3] *when condemnation,* &c. Cf. Cic. Epist. v. 2, 'qui in alios animadvertisset indictâ causâ'

[4] *broke out into those disorders.* Cf. Suet. in Ner. xxvii., 'nullâ dissimulandi curâ, ad majora vitia erupit.'

[5] *the characters they bear.* Cf. Hor. Epist. I. xvi. 17, 'tu rectè vivis si curas esse quod audis.' Also Cic. ad Att. vi. 1, 'me putant benè audire velle ut ille malè audiat.' Or turn by 'in quo numero ab inimicis habeantur.'

They either do not see our faults, or conceal them from us, or soften them[1] by their representations, after such a manner that we think them too trivial to be taken notice of.[2] An adversary, on the contrary, makes a stricter search into us, discovers every flaw and imperfection in our tempers; and though his malice[3] may set them in too strong a light, it has generally some ground for what it advances. A friend exaggerates a man's virtues, an enemy inflames his crimes. A wise man should give a just attention to both[4] of them, so far as they may tend to the improvement of the one and diminution of the other.　SPECTATOR.

LXXVI.

This was the most glorious day[5] that not only Alcibiades, but Athens herself had seen since the beginning of this unfortunate war. Whatever losses had been sustained, the people now felt elevated and comforted for their previous reverses;[6] and however much Athens had grown old and weak, yet every thing was now revived. On that day the walls and gates were guarded only by as many as were needed: all the rest of the population crowded to Piræus to receive the fleet and welcome the returning Alcibiades. He was reconciled[7] to the people; and it is no more than justice to say, that whatever tyrannical[8] inclinations may have existed in his mind before, from the moment he came to Samos he was not only a good and unpretending citizen, but a beneficial one, that he exerted himself only for good purposes, and that he was of such service to his country

---

[1] *soften them.* See Ex. XXXVII. on 'lessens their opinion of them.'

[2] *too trivial to be taken notice of.* Turn by 'leviores esse quàm ut,' or 'qui corrigantur.'

[3] *and though his malice,* &c. Turn by 'and although, if he is of a malevolent mind,' &c.

[4] *To give a just attention to both.* Cf. Cic. Epist. x. 2, 'me rationem habere velis et salutis et dignitatis meæ.'

[5] *This was the most glorious day,* &c. Turn by 'This day shone most glorious to,' &c. Cf. Cic.

Epist. i. 2, 'is dies honestissimus nobis fuerat;' and compare Horace's expression, 'pulcher ille dies risit Italiæ.' Cf. also Cic. in Pison. xv., 'qui dies reipublicæ primus illuxit.'

[6] *comforted for their reverses.* Cf. Cic. Epist. vi. 4, 'ut te consoler de miseriis communibus.'

[7] *He was reconciled.* Cf. Cic. ad Att. i. 14, 'cum Luccejo in gratiam rodi.'

[8] *whatever tyrannical,* &c. Turn by 'in animo esse regnum occupare,' or 'adfectare.'

as but few men have ever had it in their power to be. Every one at Athens was full of the brightest hopes[1] and of the joy of victory, although perhaps no one had formed any definite idea[2] of the issue of the war ; and it seems that they were only impressed with a feeling that, with the assistance of the gods, they must take courage and go on.　　　　　　　　　　　　　　　　　　Niebuhr.

LXXVII.

Both Marius and Sylla served as lieutenants[3] to the consuls in this war, and commanded separate armies in different parts of Italy ; but Marius performed nothing in it answerable to his great name and former glory—his advanced age had increased his caution ; and, after so many triumphs and consulships, he was jealous of a reverse[4] of fortune. So that he kept himself wholly on the defensive,[5] and like old Fabius, chose to tire out the enemy by declining a battle ; content with snatching some little advantages that opportunity threw into his hands, without suffering them,[6] however, to gain any against him. Sylla, on the other hand, was ever active and enterprising ; he had not yet obtained the consulship, and was fighting for it,[7] as it were, in the sight of his citizens, so that he was constantly urging the enemy to a battle, and glad of every occasion to signalize his military talents and eclipse the fame[8] of Marius.　　　　　　　　　　　　Middleton.

LXXVIII.

I know no evil under the sun so great as the abuse of the understanding, and yet there is no one vice more common. It has diffused itself through both sexes[9] and

---

[1] *full of hopes.* Cf. 'spe aliquem implere.'

[2] *no one had formed any idea,* &c. Use 'animo concipere,' and cf. Ter. And. I. ii. 5, ' verebar quorsum evaderet heri lenitas.'

[3] *served as lieutenants.* Use 'legatos stipendia facere.'

[4] *he was jealous of a reverse.* Use 'metuere ne alteram fortunam experiretur.'

[5] *To act on the defensive.* Cf. Cæs.

B. Gall. i. 44, 'defendere bellum ;' and vi. 14, ' ut injurias inferrent ipsi aut illatas propulsarent,' &c.

[6] *without suffering them,* &c. Turn by ' ipse tutus,' or 'ita tamen ut ipse nihil periclitaretur.'

[7] *fighting for it.* Use ' coram civibus quasi bellando petere.'

[8] *eclipse the fame.* Cf. Tac. Hist. ii. 32, ' nunquam obscura nomina etsi aliquando obumbrentur.'

[9] *through both sexes.* Cf. Tac.

all qualities of mankind, and there is hardly that person to be found who is not more concerned[1] for the reputation of wit and sense than honesty and virtue. But this unhappy affectation[2] of being wise rather than honest, witty than good-natured, is the source of most of the ill habits of life. Such false impressions[3] are owing to the abandoned writings of men of wit and the awkward imitation of the rest of mankind. SPECTATOR, *No.* 6.

LXXIX.

(CHANCELLOR'S MEDALS, 1848.)

Neither was he ignorant that, after he had strengthened himself with arms and a military power, neither Crassus nor Pompey could ever be able to bear up against him : whereof the one trusted[4] to his great riches, the other to his fame and reputation ; the one decayed through age, the other in power and authority, and neither of them was grounded upon true[5] and lasting foundations. And the rather for that he had obliged all the senators and magistrates, and in a word all those that had any power in the commonwealth, so firmly to himself with private benefits, that he was fearless of any combination or opposition against his designs, till he had openly invaded the imperial power ; which thing though he always bore in his mind, and at the last acted it,[6] yet he did not lay down his former person ;[7] but coloured things so, that what with[8] the reasonableness of his demands, what with his pretences of peace, and what with the moderate use of his successes,

---

Ann. iv. 62, 'virile ac muliebre secus.' Suetonius has 'uterquo sexus.'

[1] *who is not more concerned.* Use 'nemo est quin . . . pluris faciat.'

[2] *this affectation.* Turn by 'to wish to be considered . . .'

[3] *Such false impressions.* Cf. Cic. de Nat. Deor. II. ii. 25, 'opinionum commenta delet dies.'

[4] *whereof the one trusted.* If these words form part of the ideas in the man's mind, the verb must be in the subjunctive (see Introd. IV.) ;

if they are mere additions of the historian, in the indicative.

[5] *grounded on true,* &c. Cf. 'disciplina, nixa fundamento veritatis.'

[6] *and at the last acted it.* This seems a stage metaphor from the word 'person' in the next clause. Use 'in scenam inducere,' or 'in scenâ agere.'

[7] *his former person.* Cf. Cic. pro Quinc. xiii., 'personam accusatoris deponere.'

[8] *that what with,* &c. Turn by 'partim justa sibi flagitando,' &c.

he turned all the envy of the adverse party, and seemed to take up arms upon necessity for his own preservation and safety.

LXXX.

Simonides is said to have been the first who taught the art of memory. The following story respecting him is well known. Having agreed[1] for a stipulated sum to write a poem, such as was usually composed in honour of the victors at the games for a victorious athlete, a part of the payment was refused him on the ground[2] that he had digressed[3] in order to celebrate the praises of the gods, according to a poetical license by no means unusual; he was ordered therefore to obtain the other part from those whose praises he had sung: and, as the story goes, they paid him for it. For on the occasion of a great festival in honour of the victory, to which Simonides was invited, he was summoned forth by a messenger, who announced that two young men on horseback, of superhuman stature,[4] were anxiously desiring to see him. Upon going out he did not see them indeed, but found by the issue that they had not been ungrateful to him. For scarcely had he crossed the threshold, when the banqueting-hall fell with a crash upon the guests, and so crushed them that their relations, when they sought them out for burial, found no mark by which to distinguish their faces, or even the limbs of their mangled friends. Then it is said that Simonides, remembering the order in which each guest had sat down, restored the bodies to their friends.

LXXXI.

Alnaschar, says the fable, is a very idle fellow, that never would set his hand[5] to any business during his father's life. When his father died, he left him to the

---

[1] *Having agreed for a stipulated sum*, &c. Cf. 'quum pugili coronato carmen mercede pactâ scripsisset.'
[2] *on the ground that*, &c. Turn by '(saying) that he had digressed,' &c.; and 'he was ordered therefore to obtain' will be turned by the imperfect subjunctive, 'requireret

igitur:' see Ex. XIII.
[3] *To digress.* Cf. Cic. in Orat. c. xl., 'declinare aliquantulum à proposito.'
[4] *superhuman stature.* Cf. Suet., 'mortali specie amplior.'
[5] *put his hand to anything.* Use 'aggredi qd faciendum.'

value of 100 drachmas. Alnaschar, to make the best of it, laid it out [1] in glasses, bottles, and the finest earthenware. These he piled up in a large open basket at his feet, and leant [2] his back against the wall, in expectation of customers. Sitting thus, he began to meditate : "This basket," says he, "cost me at the wholesale merchant's [3] 100 drachmas ; I shall quickly make it 200 by selling it in retail : these 200 drachmas will in a very little time rise to 400, which, of course, will in time amount to 4,000 ; as soon as by this means I am master of 10,000, I will lay aside [4] my trade of glassman, and will turn jeweller." SPECTATOR.

LXXXII.

Which answer indeed had no effect. For whilst I was preparing it, studying to preserve the town from plunder, that it might be of more use to you, the captain being fairly treated yielded up the castle to us, in which our men no sooner appeared, but the enemy quitted the walls of the town ; which our men perceiving, ran violently upon the town with their ladders, and stormed it, and when they were come into the market-place, the enemy making a stiff resistance, our forces brake them, and then put all to the sword that came in their way. Two boatfuls of the enemy attempting to escape, being overprest with numbers, sank, whereby were drowned nearly 300 of them. I believe in all there was lost of the enemy not less than 2,000 ; and I believe not twenty of ours. And indeed it hath been deeply set upon our hearts,[5] that we, intending better to this place than so great a ruin, hoping the town might be of more use to you ; yet God would not have it so ; but by an unexpected providence brought

---

[1] *laid it out in.* Cf. Cic. pro Crec. iv., 'curavit ut in eo fundo dos collocaretur.'

[2] *leant*, &c. Cf. Senec. Ep. 36, 'somnus obrepere in aliquod adminiculum reclinatis.'

[3] *A wholesale merchant*, 'Mercator;' and for 'selling by retail.' cf. Tac. Ann. vi. 17, 'bonisque eorum divenditis.'

[4] *lay aside*, &c. Turn by 'becoming a jeweller, I will cease to sell glass-ware (vitrea).'

[5] *deeply set upon our hearts.* Cf. Virg. i. 466, ' mentem mortalia tangunt ;' or cf. Cic. ad Att. ix. 16, ' nequo illud me movet quod ii dicuntur,' &c.

a just judgment upon them,[1] causing *them* to become a
prey to the soldier, who had made preys of so many
families.   CROMWELL.

LXXXIII.

(CHRIST'S COLL. 1841.)

Men fear death, he said, as if unquestionably the greatest
evil: and yet no man knows that it may not be the greatest
good. If indeed great joys were in prospect, he and his
friends for him, with somewhat more reason might regret[2]
the event: but at his years[3] and with his scanty fortune,
though he was happy enough[4] at seventy still to preserve
both body and mind in vigour, yet even his present grati-
fications must necessarily soon decay. To avoid therefore
the evils of elderhood, pain, sickness, decay of sight, decay
of hearing, perhaps decay of understanding, and this by
the easiest of deaths, (for such the Athenian mode of
execution by a draught of hemlock was reputed,) and
cheered with the company of surrounding friends, could
not be otherwise than a blessing.

LXXXIV.

(CLASSICAL TRIPOS, 1841.)

It is certain the consternation[5] was very great at London,
and in the two Houses, from the time that they heard that
the King marched from Shrewsbury with a formed army,
and that he was resolved to fight[6] as soon as he could
meet with theirs. However, they endeavoured to keep
up confidently the ridiculous opinion among the common
people that the king did not command, but was carried
about in that army of the Cavaliers and was desirous to

---

[1] *brought a just judgment*, &c.
Cf. Cic. Off. ii. 8, 'jure igitur plec-
timur.' Use here 'efficere ut qs
jure' or 'merito plectatur.'

[2] *with more reason regret.* Use
the form 'quod jure queratur
habere.'

[3] *at his years.* Cf. Cic. Epist. vi.
20, 'jam id ætatis sumus.'

[4] *though he was happy enough.*

Cf. Hor. Epist. I. xvii. 36, 'non
homini cuivis contingit adire Co-
rinthum;' or use 'felici quodam
casu,' &c.

[5] *the consternation*, &c. Cf. Liv.
i. 36, 'itaque Romæ trepidatum
est.'

[6] *resolved to fight.* Cf. Liv. iv.
18, ' urbem se expugnaturos frementibus ni copia pugnæ fiat.'

escape from them : which they hoped the Earl of Essex would give him an opportunity to do. The first news they heard of the armies being engaged was by those who fled upon the first charge; who made marvellous haste from the place of danger, and thought not themselves safe, till they were gotten out of any possible danger of being pursued. It is certain, though it was past two of the clock before the battle begun, many of the soldiers and some commanders of no mean name were at St. Albans, which was near thirty miles from the field, before it was dark. These men, as all runaways do for their own excuse, reported all for lost,[1] and the king's army to be so terrible, that it could not be encountered.[2]

LXXXV.

Cicero chose the middle way[3] between the obstinacy of Cato and the indolence of Atticus; he preferred always the readiest road to what was right, if it lay open to him; if not, he took the next that seemed likely to bring him to the same end; and in politics as in morality, when he could not arrive at the true, contented himself with the probable. He oft compares the statesman to the pilot, whose art consists in managing every turn[4] of the winds, and applying even the most perverse to the progress of his voyage, so as by changing his course to arrive with safety, though later, at his destined port. He mentions likewise[5] an observation which long experience had confirmed to him, that none of the popular and ambitious who aspired to extraordinary commands and to be leaders of the re-public ever chose to obtain their ends from the people till

[1] *all for lost.* Cf. Liv. i. 47, 'jam de Servio actum rati.'

[2] *it could not be encountered.* Be careful not to use 'resisti' personally. Cf. Hirt. B. G. viii. 2, 'neque ulla magnitudine resisti posse Romanis.'

[3] *chose the middle way.* &c. Use 'quasi medium cursum tenero;' or paraphrase, 'had stripped off both

the obstinacy,' &c.; and cf. Tac. Agric. ix., 'avaritiam exuerat,' where see Walther's note.

[4] *managing every turn,* &c. Cf. Cic. Epist. i. 9, 'in navigando tempestati obsequi artis est etiam si portum tenero non queas.'

[5] *He mentions likewise,* &c. Use 'ait etiam se plurimo rerum usu expertum illud didicisse,' &c.

they had first been repulsed by the Senate.   This was verified by all their civil dissensions from the Gracchi down to Cæsar.   MIDDLETON'S *Cicero*.

LXXXVI.

The correspondence[1] of nations in that age was so imperfect and precarious that the revolutions of the north might escape the knowledge of the Court at Ravenna, till the dark cloud which was collected along the shores of the Baltic burst in thunder along the banks of the upper Danube. The emperor of the west, if his ministers disturbed his amusements[2] by the news of the impending danger, was satisfied with being the occasion and spectator of the war. The safety of Rome was intrusted to the counsels and sword[3] of Stilicho; but such was the feeble and exhausted state of the empire, that it was impossible to restore the fortifications of the Danube, or prevent by a vigorous effort the invasion of the Germans. The hopes of the vigilant minister of Honorius were confined[4] to the defence of Italy. He once more abandoned the provinces, recalled the troops, pressed the new levies which were rigorously exacted, and pusillanimously eluded, employed the most efficacious means to arrest or allure the deserters, and offered the gift of liberty and two pieces of gold[5] to all the slaves who would enlist.[6]

LXXXVII.

The temper of the people amongst whom he presides ought to be the first study[7] of a statesman; and the knowledge of this temper it is by no means impossible for

---

[1] *Correspondence was so imperfect.* Use 'commercia epistolarum' (Vell.), or 'nuntii adeò incuriosè proferebantur,' &c.

[2] *disturbed his amusements,* &c. Turn by 'if news disturbed him at leisure.' Cf. Liv. i. 6, 'intervenit his cogitationibus avitum malum.'

[3] *to the counsels and sword.* Use 'domi forisque tuendum dari,' or 'id negotii datum ut consilio et armis defenderet'

[4] *hopes were confined to.* Use 'in re aliquâ omnem spem' or 'fiduciam reponere.'

[5] *two pieces of gold.* See Ex. I.

[6] *enlist.* Cf. Liv. ii. 24, 'alius alium confirmare ne nomina darent;' also 'nomen edere,' or 'profiteri.'

[7] *ought to be the first study.* Cf. Hirt. de B. A. i., 'Cæsar maximè studebat ut partem oppidi excluderet.' For '*statesman*' use 'sena-

him to attain, if he has not an interest in being ignorant
of what it is his duty to know. To complain of the age
we live in, to murmur at the present possessors of power,
to lament the past, to conceive extravagant hopes of the
future, are the common dispositions[1] of the greatest part
of mankind, indeed the necessary effects of the ignorance
and levity of the vulgar. Such complaints have existed
in all times; yet as all times have not been alike, true
political sagacity[2] manifests itself in distinguishing that
complaint which only characterises the general infirmity
of human nature from those which are symptoms of the
particular distemperature of our own air and season.

LXXXVIII.

(CLASSICAL TRIPOS, 1850.)

The frequent commemoration of his acts was not made
so much for glory as for defence—to repel calumny, and
vindicate his measures when they were attacked: and
this is what Cicero himself declared in all his speeches,
that no man ever heard him speak[3] of himself but when
he was forced to it; that when he was urged with fictitious
crimes, it was his custom to answer them with his real
services; and if ever he said anything glorious of himself,
it was not through a fondness of praise, but to repel an
accusation; that no man who had been conversant[4] in
great affairs, and treated with particular envy, could
refute the contumely of an enemy without touching upon
his own praises; and after all his labours for the common
safety, if a just indignation[5] had drawn from him at any
time what might seem to be vain-glorious, it might reason-
ably be forgiven to him.

tor,' or 'qui rempublicam capessit,'
or 'administrat.'

[1] *are the common dispositions.*
Cf. Cic. pro Balb. xi., 'quod com-
mune est populorum liberorum non
proprium fœderatorum.'

[2] *true political sagacity.* Turn
by 'verò sapientis est,' followed by
the infinitive; or by 'he who dis-
tinguishes . . . is alone the saga-
cious politician (is demum).'

[3] *heard him speak.* Cf. Cic. pro
Domo xxxv., 'quis unquam audi-
vit quum ego dicerem.'

[4] *who had been conversant,* &c.
Cf. Cic. de Dom. xxxvi., 'vir in
magnis rebus cum invidiâ versa-
tus,' &c.

[5] *a just indignation,* &c. Cf. Cic.
de Harusp. viii., 'si animi dolor me
efferret aliquando ad gloriam.'

LXXXIX.

That when others were silent about him, if he could
not then forbear to speak of himself, that indeed would
be shameful; but when he was injured, accused, exposed
to popular odium, he must certainly be allowed to assert
his liberty, if they would not suffer him to retain his
dignity.   This, then, was the true state of the case, as it
is evident from the facts of his history; he had an ardent
love of glory, and an eager thirst of praise; was pleased,
when living, to hear his acts applauded, yet more still
with imagining that they would ever be celebrated when
he was dead; a passion[1] which, for the reasons already
hinted, had always the greatest force on the greatest souls.
But it must needs[2] raise our contempt to see every con-
ceited pedant and trifling declaimer, who know little of
Cicero's real character, and less still of their own, pre-
suming to call him the vainest of mortals.

MIDDLETON's *Cicero*, Sect. xii.

XC.

Whatever resentment Mary might feel, it did not retard
her departure from France.   She was accompanied to
Calais,[3] the place where she embarked, in a manner suitable to her dignity, as the queen of two powerful kingdoms.
Six princes of Lorraine, her uncles, with many of the most
eminent among the French nobles, were in her retinue.
Catherine, who secretly rejoiced at her departure, graced
it with every circumstance of magnificence and respect.
After bidding adieu to her mourning attendants, with a
sad heart and eyes bathed in tears,[4] Mary left that
kingdom; the short but only scene[5] of her life in which
fortune smiled upon her.   While the French coast continued in sight, she intently gazed upon it; and musing

---

[1] *a passion which.* See Ex. LXIV.

[2] *it must needs raise,* &c.   Turn
by 'those declaimers must be despised, who,' &c.; and cf. 'ludibrio et
despectui paternis inimicis erunt.'

[3] *Calais.*   Use 'portus Itius.'

[4] *eyes bathed in tears.*   Cf. Cic.
pro Sext. lxix., 'video hunc oculis
lacrymantibus me intuentem.'

[5] *the short but only scene.*   Turn
by 'where alone for a short time.'
&c.

in a thoughtful posture on that height of fortune whence she had fallen, and presaging, perhaps, the disasters and calamities which embittered the remainder of her days, she sighed often and cried out, " Farewell, France ! Farewell, beloved country, which I shall never more behold ! "[1]

XCI.

Even when the darkness of the night had hid the land from her view, she would neither retire to the cabin nor taste food ; but commanding a couch to be placed on the deck[2] she there waited for the day with the utmost impatience. Fortune soothed her on this occasion : the galley made but little way during the night. In the morning the coast of France was still within sight, and she continued to feed her melancholy with the prospect ; and as long as her eyes could distinguish it, to utter the same tender expressions of regret. At last a brisk gale arose, by the favour of which for some days, and afterwards under the cover of a thick fog, Mary escaped the English fleet, which, as she apprehended, lay in wait in order to intercept her ; and on the 19th of August, after an interval of thirteen years, landed safely at Leith in her native kingdom.[3] ROBERTSON's *Scotland*, Vol. I. Book ii.

XCII.

While the honest knight was thus bewildering himself in good starts,[4] I looked attentively upon him, which made him, I thought, collect his mind a little. " What I aim at," says he, " is to represent, that I am of opinion, to polish our understandings and neglect our manners, is of

---

[1] *which I shall never more behold.* For the order, cf. Cic. Tusc. i. 14, 'quarum baccas aspiciet ipse nunquam.'

[2] *on the deck.* Petronius has 'constratum navis;' and Tacitus, Ann. ii. 6, 'multæ pontibus stratæ,' although 'pontes' are rather; per-

haps, elevated platforms to fight from.

[3] *her native kingdom.* 'Natale solum' seems poetical (Ovid). Livy has 'solum patrium.'

[4] *in good starts.* Cf. Liv. xxii. 41, 'tumultuario prœlio ab procursu magis militum,' &c.

all things the most inexcusable.[1]   Reason should govern
passion ; but instead of that, you see, it is often sub
servient to it, and, unaccountable [2] as one would think it,
a wise man is not always a good one.   This degeneracy is
not only the guilt of particular persons, but at some times
of a whole people : and perhaps it may appear upon exa-
mination that the most polite ages are the least virtuous.
This may be attributed to the folly of admitting wit and
learning as merit in themselves, without considering [3] the
application of them.   By this means it becomes a rule
not so much to regard what we do, as how we do it.   But
this false beauty will not pass upon men of honest minds
and true tastes."

XCIII.

Sir Richard Blackmore says, with as much good sense
as virtue, " It is a mighty dishonour and shame to employ
excellent faculties and abundance of wit to humour and
please men in their vices and follies.   The great enemy of
mankind, notwithstanding his wit and angelic faculties, is
the most odious being in the whole creation."   He goes
on, soon after, to say very generously, " that he undertook the writing of his poem to rescue the Muses out of
the hands of ravishers, to restore them to their sweet and
chaste mansions, and to engage them in an employment
suitable to their dignity." [4]   This certainly ought to be
the purpose of every man who appears in public ; [5] and
whoever does not proceed upon that foundation, injures
his country as fast as he succeeds in his studies.   When
modesty ceases to be the chief ornament of one sex, and
integrity of the other, society is upon a wrong basis,[6] and

[1] *inexcusable.* Use 'nullam habet
excusationem.'
[2] *unaccountable as it may be.*
Use ' et, quod mirari licet.'
[3] *without considering.*   Turn by
' no regard being had how,' &c.;
and cf. Cic. Epist. x. 2, ' rationem
habere velis dignitatis meæ.'
[4] *suitable to their dignity.*   Cf.

Liv. xxi. 29, ' prœlium atrocius
quam pro numero pugnantium
editum.'
[5] *appears in public.*   Cf. Tac.
Hist. iv. 49, ' non in publicum
egressus est.'
[6] *on a wrong basis.*   Cf. ' in lu-
brico atque instabili fundamenta
locare' (Pliny).

we shall be ever after without rules to guide our judgment in what is really becoming[1] and ornamental. Nature and reason direct one thing, passion and humour another : to follow the dictates of the two latter, is going into a road that is both endless and intricate ; when we pursue the other, our passage is delightful, and what we aim at easily attainable.   SPECTATOR, *No.* 6.

XCIV.

Not until[2] by such treason to liberty they had lost their reputation with the mass of the nation, could he have become bold enough to attack the senators themselves. They had sold themselves[3] to become tools of his ambition, in the expectation that he would establish them as the lords of the state;[4] but after a time they found, to their disappointment, that he was resolved to be their master, and that he proved a far severer one than Servius had been. Then followed resentment and controversy, which the king suppressed by decisive violence. It is credible that the thoughtless multitude might at first rejoice at seeing retribution come on those whom it regarded as accomplices[5] in the death of king Servius. But when Tarquin's tyranny had thus cut off many eminent patricians, and terrified them all, the commonalty found too late that they had no longer any leaders, and that they could not regain their free assemblies,[6] if the king did not choose to summon them.   NEWMAN.

[1] *what is really becoming,* &c. Cf. Cic. de Off. i. 27, ' hoc loco continetur id quod dici Latino decorum potest.'

[2] *Not until by,* &c. Turn ' unless, liberty having been betrayed, they,' &c.

[3] *had sold themselves.* Use ' so vendiderant quibus ex voluntate uterentur.'

[4] *as lords of the state.* Cf. Cic. de Senec. xi., ' si dominatur in suos.'

[5] *Regard as accomplices.* Cf. Sall. in Catil. xxv., ' sæpe cædis conscia fuerat ;' also cf. Cic. pro. Cæl. xxi., ' huic facinori mens tua conscia esse non debet.'

[6] *free assemblies.* Use ' comitia.

XCV.

(CHANCELLOR'S MEDALS, 1843.)

As honours are paid to the dead in order to incite others to the imitation of their excellences, the principal intention[1] of epitaphs is to perpetuate the examples of virtue, that the tomb of a great man may supply the wants of his presence,[2] and veneration for his memory produce the same effect as the observation of his life. Those epitaphs are therefore the most perfect which set virtue in the strongest light,[3] and are best adapted to exalt the reader's ideas and rouse his emulation. To this end, it is not always necessary to recount the actions of a hero, or enumerate the writings of a philosopher. To imagine such information necessary, is to detract[4] from the character, or to suppose their works mortal, and their achievements in danger of being forgotten. The bare name of such men answers every purpose of a long inscription. Had only the name of Sir Isaac Newton been subjoined to the design upon his monument, instead of a long detail of his discoveries, which no philosopher can want, and none but a philosopher can understand, those by whose direction it was raised had done more honour both to him and themselves. This indeed is a commendation which it requires no genius to bestow, but which can never become vulgar or contemptible, if bestowed with judgment,[5] because no single age produces many men of merit superior to panegyric.

[1] *the principal intention.* Cf. Cic. Phil. xiii. 20, 'summa judicii mei spectat huc ut meorum injurias ferre possim.'

[2] *supply the wants of his presence.* Use 'ipsius operam edere,' or 'ipsius desiderium explere.' Cf. Cic. Epist. v. 8, 'ut desiderium praesentiae tuae minuatur.'

[3] *set virtue in the strongest light.* Cf. Cic. Catil. iii. 8, 'ut ea consilia illustrarentur.'

[4] *detract from.* Cf. Liv. xxxviii. 49, 'invidia detrectat virtutes.'

[5] *if bestowed with judgment.* Cf. Cic. de Fin. iii. 15, 'neque ullum delectum adhiberi oporteret.'

In consequence of this destination,[1] the validity whereof was admitted by the English, but never recognised by foreigners, Mary had reigned in England without the least complaint of neighbouring princes. But the same causes which facilitated her accession to the throne were obstacles to the elevation of her sister Elizabeth, and rendered her possession of it precarious and insecure.[2] Rome[3] trembled for the Catholic faith under a Protestant queen of such eminent abilities. The same superstitious fears alarmed the court of Spain. The impotent hatred of the Roman Pontiff, or the slow councils of Philip the Second would have produced no sudden or formidable effect. The ardent and impetuous ambition of the Princes of Lorrain, who at that time governed the court of France, was more decisive and more to be dreaded. Instigated by them, Henry, soon after the death of Mary, persuaded his daughter-in-law and her husband to assume the title of King and Queen of England. They affected to publish this to all Europe. They used that style[4] and appellation in public papers, some of which still remain. The arms of England[5] were engraved on their coin and plate and borne by them on all occasions. No preparations however were made to support this impolitic and premature claim. Elizabeth was already seated on her throne, she possessed all the intrepidity of spirit and all the arts of policy which were necessary for maintaining that station. England was growing into reputation for naval power: the marine of France had been utterly neglected;[6] and Scotland remained the only avenue by which the territories of Elizabeth could be approached.

ROBERTSON's *Scotland,* Vol. I. Book ii.

[1] *In consequence of this destination.* Uso 'cujus auctoritatis jure.'

[2] *precarious and insecure.* Cf. Tac. Hist. i. 52, 'precarium seni imperium.'

[3] *Rome.* Uso 'Pontifex maximus;' and for 'a Protestant queen,' uso 'regina in verba aliena jurata.'

[4] *They used that style,* &c. Cf. Tac. Ann. i. 7, 'ne edictum quidem nisi tribuniciæ potestatis præscriptione posuit.'

[5] *arms of England.* Uso 'insignia imperii Britannici.'

[6] *neglected.* Cf. Cic. Off. iii. 20, 'Marius post præturam jacebat.'

XCVII.

(St. John's College, 1859.)

The king had cast the business thus with himself. He took it for granted in his own judgment that the war of Brittaine, in respect of the strength of the towns and of the party, could not speedily[1] come to a period. So then judging it would be a work of time, he laid his plot how he might best make use of that time for his own affairs. Wherein first he thought to make his vantage[2] upon his Parliament, knowing that they being affectionate unto the quarrel of Brittaine would give treasure largely. Which treasure as a noise of war might draw forth, so a peace succeeding might coffer up. And because he knew his people were hot upon the business, he chose rather to seem to be deceived and lulled to sleep by the French than to be backward in himself; considering his subjects were not so fully capable of the reasons of the state[3] which made him hold back. Wherefore to all these purposes he saw no other expedient than to set and keep on foot a continual treaty of peace, laying it down and taking it up again as the occurrence required.   Lord Bacon.

XCVIII.

When we are considering how history should be read, the main thing perhaps is, that the person reading should desire to know what he is reading about, not merely to have read the books that tell of it. The most elaborate and careful historian must omit, or pass slightly over, many parts of his subject. He writes for all[4] readers,

[1] *could not speedily*, &c. Cf. Liv. xxi. 40, 'cum ruptore fœderum deos ipso committere ac profligare bellum.'

[2] *to make his vantage.* Cf. Cic. de Off. ii. 22, 'Habere enim quæstui rempublicam turpe est;' or use 'ut senatores sibi lucro forent:' where observe that 'sibi' refers to the main subject of the sentence, not the subject of the subsidiary clause,

contrary to strict rule, but in accordance with the general usage.

[3] *reasons of the state.* Cf. Tac. Hist. i. 4, 'evulgato arcano imperii.'

[4] *He writes for all*, &c. Use 'in universorum commodum;' and for the next words, cf. Tac. Hist. i. 46, 'omnia deinde arbitrio militum acta.'

and cannot indulge private fancies. But history has its particular aspect[1] for each man : there must be portions which he may be expected to dwell upon. And everywhere, even where the history is most laboured, the reader should have something of the spirit of research which was needful for the writer : if only so much as to ponder well the words of the writer.

FRIENDS IN COUNCIL, vol. i. p. 231.

XCIX.

The king was alarmed[2] at the yoke which he saw prepared for him. Buckingham's sole guilt,[3] he thought, was the being his friend and favourite. All the other complaints against him were mere pretences. A little before he was the idol of the people.[4] No new crime had since been discovered. After the most diligent inquiry, the smallest appearance of guilt could not be fixed upon him. What idea, he asked, must all mankind entertain of his honour, should he sacrifice[5] his innocent friend to pecuniary considerations ? What further authority should he retain in the nation, were he capable, in the beginning of his reign,[6] to give, in so signal an instance, such matter of triumph[7] to his enemies and discouragement to his adherents ?

C.

Good nature is more agreeable in conversation than wit, and gives a certain air[8] to the countenance which is more amiable than beauty. It shews virtue[9] in the fairest light,

[1] *has its aspects.* Use ' Prout cuique libido est accipere.'

[2] *The king was alarmed.* Turn, ' The king (began) to fear lest a yoke,' &c.; and cf. the phrases, ' sub jugum mittere,' ' jugum ei imponere,' &c.

[3] *sole guilt.* Use 'id vitio dari,' or ' esse in crimine.'

[4] *idol of the people.* Cf. Cicero's phrase, ' esse in amore et deliciis alicui.'

[5] *sacrifice his friend.* Use ' ami-

cum lucro posthabere.'

[6] *in the beginning of his reign.* Use ' inter initia regni,' or ' primis imperii diebus.'

[7] *such matter of triumph.* Cf. Cic. de Amic. xvi., ' quo plures det tanquam ansas ad reprehendendum.'

[8] *Give an air.* Use ' nescio qd addere.'

[9] *shews virtue,* &c. Use 'qd commendare,' or ' qd illustrare.'

takes off in some measure from the deformity of vice, and makes even folly and impertinence supportable. There is no society or conversation to be kept up in the world without good nature, or something which must bear its appearance and supply its place.[1] For this reason mankind have been forced to invent a kind of artificial humanity, which is what we express[2] by the word "good-breeding." For if we examine thoroughly the idea of what we call so, we shall find it to be nothing else but an imitation and mimicry of good nature, or, in other terms, affability and easiness of temper reduced into an art.[3]

SPECTATOR.

CI.

(CLASSICAL TRIPOS, 1848.)

Having given the ambassador his hand to kiss, and inquired of the queen's health,[4] he willed him to go sit in the place provided for him, nigh ten paces distant, from thence to send him the queen's letters and present; which the ambassador thinking not reasonable stepped forward; but the chancellor meeting him, would have taken his letters; to whom the ambassador said that the queen had directed no letters to him; and so went on and delivered them to the emperor's own hands. And after a short withdrawing into the council-chamber, where he had conference with some of the council, he was called in to dinner; about the midst[5] whereof the emperor, standing up, drank a deep carouse[6] to the queen's health, and sent to the ambassador a great bowl of Rhenish wine to pledge him.

[1] *supply its place.* Cf. Tac. Ann. iv. 8, 'vestram meamque vicem explete,' or 'vices obire.'

[2] *what we express.* Cf. Plinius xvi. 16, 'tertium genus nostrates vocant silvestre.' For 'good-breeding' use 'urbanitas.'

[3] *reduced into an art.* Use 'in artem redigi,' or 'in modum artis venire.'

[4] *of the queen's health.* 'Valetudo' alone is ambiguous, and depends for its meaning on the context. Turn by 'whether the queen enjoyed good health;' and cf. the phrase of Nepos, 'tantâ prosperitate usus valetudinis,' &c.

[5] *about the midst.* Cf. Cic. ad Q. F. iii. 1, 'hæc inter cœnam puero dictavi,' or 'inter cœnandum.'

[6] *drank a deep carouse,* &c. Cf. 'Propino tibi salutem plenis faucibus.' (Plaut. Stich. III. ii. 15); and 'propino hoc pulcro Critiæ (Cic. Tusc. i. 40), for the construction.

CII.

(Caius College, 1847.)

If therefore thou fallest from thy employment[1] in
public, take sanctuary in an honest retirement, being
indifferent[2] to thy gain abroad, or thy safety at home.   If
thou art out of favour with thy prince, secure the favour
of the King of kings,[3] and then there is no harm come to
thee.   And when Zeno Cittiensis lost all his goods in a
storm, he retired to the studies of philosophy, to his short
cloak[4] and a severe life, and gave thanks to fortune for his
prosperous mischance.   When the north wind blows hard
and it rains sadly, none but fools sit down in it and cry ;
wise people defend themselves against it with a warm gar-
ment, or a good fire and a dry roof.   When the storm of
a sad mischance beats upon our spirits, turn it to some
advantage[5] by observing where it can serve another end
either of religion or prudence ; it will turn into something
that is good, if we list to make it so.

CIII.

(King's College, 1841.)

He endeavoured to prove the motion made by Bell to
be a vain device, and perilous to be treated of, since it
tended to[6] the derogation of the prerogative imperial ;
which, whoever would attempt so much as in fancy, could
not be said to be otherwise accounted than an open enemy.
For what difference is there between saying that the queen

[1] *fallest from thy employment.*
Cf. Curt. x. 5, 'so iterum captas,
iterum excidisse regno.'

[2] *indifferent to thy gain,* &c. Cf.
Tac. Hist. iii. 41, 'apud dedecoris
securos ;' and cf. Virg. i. 354, 'so-
curus amorum germanae.'

[3] *the King of kings.* Cf. Hor.
iii. 1, ' Reges in ipsos imperium
est Jovis.'

[4] *his short cloak.* Cf. Juv. iii.
115, 'Audi facinus majoris abollæ.'

[5] *turn it to some advantage.* Cf.
Cic. de Off. ii. 22, ' habere enim
quæstui non modo turpe est ;' and
for the next words, turn by ' when
you have perceived whether you
can derive other profit,' &c.

[6] *tended to,* &c. Use 'eò spectare
ut jus regium imminueretur.'

is not to use the privilege of the crown,[1] and saying that
she is not queen ? And though experience has shown so
much clemency in her majesty as might perhaps make
subjects forget their duty, it is not good to sport or venture
too much with princes.

CIV.

He reminded them [2] of the fable of the hare, who, upon
proclamation that the horned beasts should depart the
court immediately, fled, lest his ears should be construed
into horns. And by his apologue he seems to insinuate
that even those who heard or permitted such dangerous
speeches would not themselves be entirely free from danger.
He desired them to beware, lest if they meddled [3] with
these matters further, the queen might look to her own
power, and finding herself able to repress the challenged
liberty, and to exert an arbitrary authority,[4] might imitate
the example of Louis of France, who, as he termed it,
delivered the crown from wardship.

CV.

The conspirators determined to make their attack upon
him as soon as he should enter the assembly. Among the
floating stories [5] of the day was a prediction that the Ides
of March should be fatal to Cæsar.[6] It appears that he
had received intimations from more than one quarter of
the danger which threatened him : but he resolutely
rejected all advice to guard himself against it, relying, as

[1] *privilege of the crown.* Avoid
'privilegium,' which properly
means a law passed with reference
to a single person, usually against
him. Use 'regia auctoritas,' or
'potestas,' &c.

[2] *He reminded them,* &c. Turn
by the oratio obliqua imperative.
Cf. Liv. ii. 24, 'cum omnibus potius
quam solos perituros ; patres mili-
tarent,' &c.

[3] *Meddle with.* Cf. Cic. Epist.
x. 27, 'sapientius facies si te in

istam pacificationem non interpo-
nes,' or 'se immisceri ei rei.'

[4] *exert arbitrary authority,* 'suo
jure uti,' or 'ex libidine agere.'
Cf. Tac. Ann. iv. 46, 'ne regibus
quidem parere nisi ex libidine
soliti.'

[5] *Among the floating,* &c. Use
'inter alia tum maxime vulgata.'

[6] *should be fatal to Cæsar.* Cf.
Cic. in Catil. iii. 4, 'hic annus fa-
talis est ad interitum,' &c.

he declared, implicitly on the good sense or gratitude of the citizens. It had long been[1] the fixed principle of his philosophy that the only way[2] to enjoy life was to banish the fear of death. On the eve[3] of the fatal day he was entertained by Lepidus; and when, in the course of conversation, some one started the question, what kind of death is the best, it was remarked[4] that he cut short the discussion abruptly with the reply, "That which is least expected." MERIVALE.

CVI.

While awaiting the arrival of the dictator, Brutus and Cassius occupied themselves, as prætors, with listening to casual applications;[5] and the freedom with which the former expressed himself, rebuking those who boasted that Cæsar would reverse his decisions,[6] was especially remarked. But as the morning wore on, the conspirators were exposed to redoubled risks. A senator, addressing Casca with a significant smile, said, "You have concealed your secret from me, but Brutus has revealed it." In another moment, Casca would have pressed his hand and communicated the dark design; but the other went on to allude[7] to his meditated competition for the ædileship, and the conspirator saw that he was undiscovered. Læna whispered to Brutus,[8] "What you have in hand despatch quickly," and was immediately lost in the crowd. MERIVALE.

[1] *It had long been*, &c. Cf. Cic. in Verr. vii. 25, 'Hodieque omnes sic habent persuasum, istum,' &c.

[2] *the only way to*, &c. Turn by 'the fear of death being removed, then only it was possible,' &c. Cf. Plinius vii. 7, 'is demum vitam pensitabit qui fragilitatis humanæ memor fuerit.'

[3] *On the eve of.* Cf. Tac. xv. 54, 'Pridie insidiarum testamentum obsignavit;' and 'pridie constitutam diem:' also Cic. Epist. v. 11, 'pridie quam Athenas veni.'

[4] *it was remarked that*, &c. Cf. Cic. ad Att. iii. 23, 'in lege nulla esse capita to non fallit:' and for

the next words, cf. Liv. xxxii. 37, 'brevis interrogatio sermonem incidit:' also 'sermonem abrumpere' is used.

[5] *listening to casual applications.* Use 'forte litigantibus jura dare.'

[6] *reverse his decisions.* Cf. Cic. Phil. xi. 5, 'quorum res judicatas irritas fecimus.'

[7] *went on to allude to,* &c. Use 'de ædilitatis petitione verba facere.' Be careful not to use 'verba dare;' which means to 'impose on.'

[8] *whispered to Brutus.* Cf. Cic. in Verr. vii. 41, 'Eum vident ad aures familiariter insusurrare.'

CVII.

The constant tradition[1] of antiquity declared that, among many prognostics of an impending catastrophe, his wife had revealed to him in the morning an ominous dream, and when she prevailed upon him to consult the sacrificers, the signs of the victims[2] were fearfully inauspicious. Whether his own superstitious[3] feelings gained the ascendancy, or whether he was overcome by the entreaties of Calpurnia, he consented at last to send Antonius to dismiss the senate, or to excuse his absence. At this moment Decimus Brutus came to attend him on his way to the place of meeting. When he heard the dictator's half blushing acknowledgement[4] of his scruples, he was struck with consternation at the prospect of the destined victim's escape;[5] for in the meanwhile the conspirators were in momentary apprehension[6] of discovery. Brutus himself, tormented by fear or conscience, had been unable to conceal his agitation since he had embarked in the enterprise, and his nervous excitement was shamed by the firmness of his wife, who pierced her own thigh, and long concealed the wound, to extract from him the secret of his heart.[7]   MERIVALE.

CVIII.

It is an endless and frivolous pursuit to act by any other rule than the care of satisfying our own minds in what we do. One would think a silent man, who con-

[1] *The constant tradition,* &c. Turn by 'illud ferè inter auctores constat.'

[2] *the signs of the victims,* &c. Cf. Suet. in Cæsar. lxxxi., 'Pluribus victimis cæsis quum litare non posset;' or simply use 'omina tristissima esse.'

[3] *his own superstitious,* &c. Turn by 'moved either by religion or by the prayers,' &c.

[4] *the dictator's half blushing,* &c. Use 'pudenter excusare superstitionem,' or 'se excusare quod superstitione obligaretur.'

[5] *of the destined victim's escape.* Use 'ne is quem interfecturi erant evaderet,' &c.

[6] *in momentary apprehension.* Cf. Hor. Od. ii. 13, 'nunquam homini satis cautum est in horas.'

[7] *extract the secret of his heart.* Cf. Senec. Hipp. 884, 'secreta mentis extrahere;' and also Tac. Ann. vi. 3, 'omnium secreta rimantem.'

cerned himself with no one breathing, [1] should be very
little liable to misinterpretations; and yet, I remember
I was once taken up for a Jesuit, [2] for no other reason but
my profound taciturnity. It is from this misfortune that,
to be out of harm's way, I have ever since affected crowds.
He who comes into assemblies only to gratify his curiosity,
and not to make a figure, enjoys the pleasures of retirement in a more exquisite degree than he possibly could in
his closet: the lover, the ambitious, and the miser, are
followed thither by a worse crowd than any they can with-
draw from. To be exempt from the passions with which
others are tormented, is the only pleasing [3] solitude. I can
very justly say with the ancient sage, I am "never less
alone than when alone." SPECTATOR, *No.* 4.

CIX.

As I am insignificant [4] to the company in public places,
and as it is visible I do not come thither, as most do, to
show myself, I gratify the vanity of all who pretend to
make an appearance, [5] and have often as kind looks from
well dressed gentlemen and ladies as a poet would bestow
upon one of his audience. There are so many gratifica-
tions attend this public sort of obscurity, that some little
distastes I daily receive have lost their anguish; and I did
the other day, without the least displeasure, overhear one
say of me, "That strange fellow;" and another answer,
"I have known the fellow's face [6] these twelve years, and
so must you; but I believe you are the first ever asked
who he was." There are, I must confess, many to whom
my person is as well known as that of their nearest rela-

---

[1] *with no one breathing.* Virgil,
Æn. i. 546, has 'si vescitur aurâ
ætheriâ;' and 'vitales carpere au-
ras.' If this is poetical, use 'homines quotquot vivunt.'

[2] *taken up for a Jesuit.* Use
'tanquam Jesuitam in carcerem
dari,' or 'mitti,' or 'in custodiâ
teneri.'

[3] *is the only pleasing,* &c. Cf.
Sall. Cat. xx., 'idem velle atque

nolle ea demum firma amicitia est.'

[4] *insignificant.* Cf. Cic. Phil. iii.
6, 'homo nullo numero;' also cf.
the phrase, 'aliquem numerum
obtinere.'

[5] *to make an appearance.* Cf.
Cic. ad Att. ii. 23, 'ceteris præ se
fert et ostentat.'

[6] *known the fellow's face.* Cf.
Cic. in Pison. xxxii., 'tu virtutem
ne de facie quidem nosti.'

tions, who give themselves no farther trouble about calling me by my name or quality, but speak of me very currently by " Mr. What-do-ye-call-him." [1]   SPECTATOR, *No.* 4.

CX.

It may not be unacceptable to the reader to see how Sophocles has conducted a tragedy under the like delicate circumstances. Orestes was in the same condition [2] with Hamlet in Shakspeare; his mother having murdered his father, and taken possession of the kingdom in conspiracy with the adulterer. That young prince, therefore, being determined to revenge his father's [3] death upon those that filled his throne, conveys himself by a beautiful stratagem into his mother's apartment, with a resolution to kill her. But because such a spectacle would have been too shocking for the audience, his dreadful resolution is executed behind the scenes : the mother is heard calling out to her son for mercy, and the son answering her that she showed no mercy to his father ; after which she shrieks out that she is wounded, and by what follows we find that she is slain.

SPECTATOR, *No.* 44.

CXI.

I do not remember that in any of our plays there are speeches made behind the scenes, though there are other instances of this nature to be met with in those of the ancients; and I believe the reader will agree with me, that there is something infinitely more affecting [4] in this dreadful dialogue between the mother and her son behind the scenes, than could have been in anything transacted before the audience. Orestes, immediately after, meets the usurper at the entrance of his palace, and, by a very

---

[1] *Mr. What-do-ye-call-him.* Use ' me quolubet vocabulo appellare.'

[2] *was in the same condition.* Cf. Ter. Adelph. III. ii. 45, ' pejore res loco non potis esse quàm in hoc quo nunc sita est.'

[3] *to revenge his father's.* Cf

Cic. ad Att. i. 16, ' pœnas ab optimo quoque peteret sui doloris.'

[4] *something more affecting.* Cf. Cic. de Orat. ii. 47, ' non prius conatus sum misericordiam aliis commovere, quàm ipse misericordiâ captus sum.'

happy thought [1] of the poet, avoids killing him before the audience, that he should live some time in his present bitterness of soul before he would despatch him, and by ordering him to retire into that part of the palace where he had slain his father, whose murder he would revenge in the very same place where it was committed. By this means the poet observes that decency,[2] which Horace afterwards established by a rule, of forbearing to commit parricides or unnatural murders before the audience.

> "Let not Medea with unnatural rage,
> Slaughter her mangled infants on the stage."

SPECTATOR, No. 44.

CXII.

Darkness and light divide the course of time,[3] and oblivion [4] shares with memory a great part even of our living beings : we slightly remember our felicities, and the smartest strokes of affliction leave but short smart upon us. Sense endureth no extremities, and sorrows destroy us or themselves. To weep into stones are fables. Afflictions induce callosities,[5] miseries are slippery, or fall like snow upon us, which, notwithstanding, is no unhappy stupidity. To be ignorant of evils to come, and forgetful of evils past, is a merciful provision in nature, whereby we digest the mixture [6] of our few and evil days, and our delivered senses not relapsing into cutting remembrances, our sorrows are not kept raw [7] by the edge of repetitions.

SIR THOMAS BROWNE.

[1] *a very happy thought.* Use 'felicissimâ arte poetæ.'

[2] *that decency.* Use 'decorum,' or 'id quod decet' (Cic. de Off. i. 27).

[3] *divide the course,* &c. Cf. Plaut. Aul. II. iv. 3, 'ut dispartirem obsonium hic bifariam.'

[4] *oblivion shares,* &c. Turn by 'give as much to oblivion as to memory.'

[5] *induce callosities.* Cf. Plaut. Pseud. I. ii. 4, 'costæ plagis callent.'

[6] *digest the mixture.* Cf. Liv. iv. 15, 'quem senatorem concoquere civitas vix posset ;' and Tac. Hist. i. 10, 'bonis malisque artibus mixtus.'

[7] *kept raw.* Cf. Cic. Epist. iv. 6,

CXIII.

I cannot praise a fugitive and cloistered[1] virtue, un-exercised and unbreathed,[2] that never sallies out and sees her adversary, but slinks out of the race where that immortal garland is to be run for,[3] not without dust and heat. Assuredly we bring not innocence into the world, we bring impurity rather ; that which purifies us is trial, and trial is by what is contrary. That virtue, therefore, which is but a youngling in the contemplation of evil, and knows not the utmost that vice promises to her followers and rejects it, is but a blank virtue, not a pure ; which was the reason why our sage and serious poet Spenser (whom I dare be known to think a better teacher than Scotus or Aquinas), describing[4] true temperance under the person of Guion, brings him with his palmer through the Cave of Memnon and the bower of earthly bliss, that he might see and know, and yet abstain.   MILTON.

CXIV.

(CLARE COLLEGE, 1850.)

We are always resolving to live, and yet never set about life[5] in good earnest. Archimedes was not singular in his fate : but a great part of mankind die unexpectedly, while they are poring upon the figures they have described in the sand. O wretched mortals, who, having condemned themselves, as it were, to the mines,[6] seem to make it their chief study to prevent their ever gaining their liberty.[7]

'illa quæ consanuisse videbantur recrudescunt.'

[1] *cloistered.* Use 'quasi parietibus septus.'

[2] *unbreathed,* 'anhelitûs expers.'

[3] *is to be run for.* Use 'proponi quod cursores auferant.'

[4] *describing temperance.* Cf. Cic. de Orat. c. ii., 'talem informabo qualis nemo unquam fuit;' and for the next words, cf. Cic. Tusc. v. 39, ' Teiresiam nunquam inducunt deplorantem cæcitatem suam,' turn-ing by ' brings him forward as journeying,' &c.

[5] *set about life in earnest.* Cf. Cic. ad Att. xvi. 10, 'totâ mente incumbe in hanc curam.'

[6] *Condemn to the mines,* 'in metalla damnare.' (Suet.)

[7] *Gain their liberty.* Cf. Cic. Epist. ii. 5, 'rempublicam in libertatem vindicaturus.' Also cf. Cæs. B. G. vii. 6, ' libertatis vindicandæ.'

Hence new employments are assumed in the place of old
ones; one hope succeeds another,[1] one instance of ambition makes way for another; and we never desire an end
to our misery, but only that it may change its outward
form. When we cease to be candidates, and to fatigue
ourselves in soliciting interest,[2] we begin to give our votes
and interest to those who solicit us in their turn. When
we are weary of the trouble of prosecuting crimes at the
bar, we commence judges ourselves; and he who is grown
old in the management of other men's affairs for money is
at last employed in improving his own wealth.

CXV.

Ah! we will have no more about Sunday schools.[3] I
know we all agree in reality, although Dunsford has been
looking very grave,[4] and has not said a word. I wanted
to tell you that I think you are quite right in saying a
good deal about multifariousness[5] of pursuit. You see
a wretch of a pedant[6] who knows all about tetrameters,
or statutes of uses,[7] but who, as you hinted an essay or
two ago, can hardly answer his child a question as they
walk about the garden together. The man has never
given a good thought[8] or look to nature. Well then,
again, what a stupid thing it is, that we are not all taught
music. Why learn the language of many portions of
mankind, and leave the universal language[9] of the feelings, as you would call it, unlearnt?

FRIENDS IN COUNCIL, I. 176.

---

[1] *one hope succeeds another.* Cf.
Hor. ii. 18, 'truditur dies die.'

[2] *soliciting interest,* ' prensare,
ambire;' and for 'giving our vote.'
&c., cf. Cic. Epist. x. 7, 'A te peto
ut dignitati meæ suffrageris.' Pliny
has also ' candidatum suffragio
ornare.'

[3] *about Sunday schools.* Use ' de
pueris instituendis.'

[4] *has been looking very grave.*
Cf. Tac. Hist. i. 82, ' miles in obsequium compositus.'

[5] *multifariousness,* &c. Turn by

' studies extending widely.'

[6] *a wretch of a pedant,* &c. Use
' inepti sunt qui,' &c.

[7] *statutes of uses.* Cf. Cic. pro
Cæc. vii., ' usus et fructus fundi
fuerat Cæsenniæ.'

[8] *given a good thought,* &c. Cf.
Sall. Catil. xii., ' pudorem nihil
pensi habere.'

[9] *universal language,* &c. Turn
by ' that language by which the
feelings are expressed universally'
(' in universum ').

G

CXVI.

MILVERTON.—I quite agree with you; but I thought you always set your face,[1] or rather your ears, against music.

ELLESMERE.—I should like to know all about it. It is not to my mind that a cultivated man should be quite thrown out[2] by any topic of conversation, or that there should be any form of human endeavour, of accomplishment, which he has no conception of.

DUNSFORD.—I liked what you said, Milverton, about the philosophy of making light of little things, and the way of looking at life that may thus be given to those we educate. I rather doubted at first, though, whether you were not going to assign too much[3] power to education in the modification of temper. But, certainly, the mode of looking[4] at the daily wants of life, little or great, and the consequent habits of captiousness, or magnanimity, are just the matters which the young especially imitate their elders in.   FRIENDS IN COUNCIL, I. 177.

CXVII.

I cannot tell whether I am to account him whom I am next to speak of as one of our company; for he visits us but seldom, but when he does, it adds to every man else a new enjoyment[5] of himself. He is a clergyman, a very philosophic man, of general learning, great sanctity of life, and the most exact good breeding. He has the misfortune[6] to be of a very weak constitution;[7] and conse-

---

[1] set your face, &c. Cf. Cic. in Verr. vii. 55, 'qui nunc animo te iniquissimo infestissimoque intuetur.'

[2] thrown out. Cf. 'se iterum captas iterum excidisse regno.'

[3] assign too much power, &c. Use 'nimium institutioni tribuere.'

[4] But, certainly, the mode, &c. Turn by 'with what feeling the young hear . . . . so as to turn out . . . . they are taught.'

[5] adds a new enjoyment, &c. Use 'facere ut quisque amore sui novo teneatur.'

[6] He has the misfortune, &c. Turn by 'Casu quodam infelici,' or 'In eâ parte infelix est quod,' &c.

[7] to be of a very weak constitution. 'Valetudo' means either good or bad health, and generally takes an adjective to determine it; as 'valetudine minus commodâ uti,' 'optimâ valetudine uti,' &c.

quently cannot accept of such cares[1] and business as preferments in his function would oblige him to : he is, therefore, among divines what a chamber counsellor[2] is among lawyers. The probity of his mind and the integrity of his life create him followers, as being eloquent or loud advances others. He seldom introduces the subjects he speaks upon ; but we are so far gone in years, that he observes when amongst us an earnestness to have him fall on some divine topic, which he always treats with much authority, as one who has no interests in this world, as one who is hastening to the object[3] of all his wishes, and conceives hopes from his decays and infirmities. These are my ordinary companions. SPECTATOR, *No.* II.

CXVIII.

When the queen's counsel had finished, Mary stood up, and with great magnanimity and equal presence of mind began her defence. She bewailed[4] the unhappiness of her own situation, that, after a captivity of nineteen years, during which she had suffered treatment no less cruel than unmerited, she was at last loaded with an accusation which tended[5] not only to rob her of the right of succession,[6] and to deprive her of life itself, but to transmit her name with infamy to future ages ; that without regarding the sacred rites of sovereignty, she was now subjected to laws framed against private persons, though an anointed queen,[7] commanded to appear before the tribunal of subjects, and, like a common criminal,[8] her honour exposed to the petulant tongues of lawyers capable of wresting her

[1] *accept of such cares*, &c. Turn by ' is unequal to duties such as are those of all who obtain preferment,' &c.

[2] *chamber counsellor*, &c. Use 'inter causidicos jure consultus.'

[3] *hastening to the object*, &c. Cf. Suet. in Aug. lviii., 'compos factus meorum votorum.'

[4] *She bewailed*, &c. Turn by ' that her lot was miserable, who,' &c.

[5] *which tended not only to*, &c.

Cf. ' spectare ad bene beateque vivendum.'

[6] *right of succession.* Tacitus has 'jura successionum' (Germ. xxxii.), although the word is rare. Or use 'regnum' alone.

[7] *though an anointed queen.* Cf. Liv. ix. 8, ' neque, quum sacrosancti essent, dedi hostibus violare posse.'

[8] *a common criminal.* Use ' tanquam de plebe rea quævis.'

words, and of misrepresenting her actions; that even in this dishonourable situation [1] she was denied the privileges usually granted to criminals, and obliged to undertake her own defence, without the presence of any friend with whom to advise, without the aid of counsel, and without the use of her own papers.

ROBERTSON's Scotland, II. Book vii.

CXIX.

In order to save her from this cruel mortification, he applied to Maitland,[2] and expressed his astonishment at seeing a man of so much reputation for wisdom concurring with the regent in a measure so dishonourable to themselves and their queen, submitting the public transactions of the nation to the judgment of foreigners.[3] It was easy for Maitland, whose sentiments were the same as the duke's, to vindicate his own conduct. He assured him that he had employed all his credit to dissuade his countrymen from the measure, and would still contribute to the utmost of his power to divert them from it. This encouraged Norfolk to communicate [4] the matter to the regent. He repeated and enforced the same arguments which he had used with Maitland. He warned him of the danger to which he must expose himself by such a violent action as the public accusation of his sovereign. Mary would never forgive a man who had endeavoured to fix such a brand [5] of infamy on her character. If she ever recovered any degree of power, his destruction [6] would be inevitable, and he would justly merit it at her hands. Nor would Elizabeth screen him from this by a public appro-bation of his conduct. For whatever evidence of Mary's guilt he might produce, she was resolved to give no

---

[1] *in this dishonourable*, &c. Cf. Cæs. B. G. ii. 22, 'in tantâ rerum iniquitate.'

[2] *applied to Maitland, and expressed.* Turn by 'Maitlando adito se mirari,' omitting the word 'said,' or the like, as usual.

[3] *to the judgment of foreigners.*

Use 'ad arbitrium aliorum vivere,' or 'qd arbitrio es permittere.'

[4] *communicate.* Cf. Cic. ad Att. i. 18, 'quîcum omnia communicem.' The dative is much less common.

[5] *fix such a brand.* See Ex. LIV.

[6] *destruction*, &c. Use 'jure exitium certum fore.'

definite sentence in the cause. Let him only demand that the matter should be brought to a decision[1] immediately after hearing the proof, and he would be fully convinced how false and invidious her intentions were, and by consequence how improper it would be for him to appear as the accuser of his own sovereign.

ROBERTSON'S *Scotland*, Book v.

CXX.

(CLASSICAL TRIPOS, 1858.)

If we estimate the character of a sovereign by the test of popular affection, we must rank Edward among the best princes of his time. The goodness of his heart was adored by his subjects, who lamented his death with tears of undissembled grief, and bequeathed his memory as an object of veneration to their posterity. The blessings of his reign are the constant theme[2] of our ancient writers; not indeed that he displayed any of those brilliant qualities which attract attention while they inflict misery. He could not boast of the victories which he had won, or of the conquests which he had achieved; but he exhibited the interesting spectacle[3] of a king negligent of his private interests, and totally devoted to the welfare of his people. To him the principle that the king can do no wrong was literally applied by the gratitude of the people, who, if they occasionally complained of the measures of the government, attributed the blame not to the monarch himself, of whose benevolence they entertained no doubt, but to the ministers who had abused his confidence[4] or deceived his credulity. Writers were induced to view his character with more partiality from the hatred with which they looked on his successors and predecessors. They

[1] *matter brought to a decision.* Use 'litem dijudicare.'

[2] *are the constant theme.* Cf. Cic. in Cat. iv. 10, 'memoria . . . in omnium gentium sermonibus semper hærebit.' Or use ' continuis laudibus tollere,' or ' efferro.'

[3] *the interesting spectacle.* Cf.

Cic. ad Att. x. 2, 'homini non amico nostra incommoda spectaculo esse nollem.'

[4] *abused his confidence, &c.* Turn by 'either little faitbful or rashly listened to;' and observe that 'creditus' used personally in this sense is only poetical.

were foreigners, he was a native ; they held the crown by conquest, he by descent ; they ground to the dust[1] the slaves whom they had made, he became known to his countrymen only by his benefits.

CXXI.

Who is to furnish the materials from which the philosopher of a future age shall draw his lessons[2] of practical wisdom ? Are the virtues alone and not the vices of man to be recorded ? Is the chronicler of his own times to be a mere composer of panegyric ?[3] Shall he describe a golden age of happiness, which, in the iron days that follow, the sad experience[4] of mankind will force them to disbelieve ? Shall he leave to his successor the laborious task of unravelling a tissue[5] of misrepresentation,—and if so, at what period shall truth begin ? Shall it commence with the epitaph ? Or must the dead still be honoured to spare the feelings of the living ? It cannot be ; no man may hope to escape the sentence of his fellows. High or low, it is the same ; the villager receives a character from his neighbours, the statesman from his country.

CXXII.

(CLASSICAL TRIPOS, 1836.)

He that goeth about to persuade a multitude that they are not so well governed as they ought to be, shall never want attentive[6] and favourable hearers ; because they know the manifold defects whereunto every kind of regiment is subject ; but the secret lets and difficulties, which in public

---

[1] *ground to the dust.* Cf. Tac. Ann. xv. 11, 'vi ac minis alares exterruit, legionarios obtrivit.'

[2] *draw lessons of wisdom.* Use 'exemplis prudentiæ instrui.'

[3] *a mere composer of panegyric.* Cf. Cic. Epist. ix. 14, 'te summis laudibus ad cœlum extulerunt.'

[4] *the sad experience,* &c. Turn by 'which amongst men experiencing different things will hardly

meet with credit ;' and cf. Liv. ix. 36, 'abhorrebat a fide quenquam,' &c.

[5] *unravelling a tissue,* &c. Cf. Cic. Acad. iv. 29, 'quasi Penelopæ texam retexens.'

[6] *attentive hearers,* &c. Cf. Cic. ad Att. xvi. 2, 'bonos auditores nactus.' Or use 'apud æquos concionari,' or 'pronis auribus accipi' (Tac. Hist. I. i.), or similar phrase.

proceedings are innumerable, they have not ordinarily the judgment to consider. And because such as openly reprove supposed disorders of state are taken for principal friends to the common benefit of all, and for men that carry singular freedom of mind;[1] under this fair and plausible colour, whatsoever they utter passeth for good and current.[2] That which wanteth in the weight of their speech, is supplied by the aptness of men's minds to accept and believe it.   HOOKER.

CXXIII.

(BELL'S SCHOLARSHIP, 1848.)

I will now mention the favourable opportunity which you have, if you wish to embrace it, of obliging foreigners, among whom there is no one at all conspicuous for genius or for elegance who does not make the Tuscan language[3] his delight, and indeed consider it as an essential part of education, particularly if he be only slightly tinctured[4] with the literature of Greece or of Rome. I, who certainly have not merely wetted the tip[5] of my lips in the stream of those languages, but, in proportion to my years, have swallowed the most copious draughts, can yet sometimes retire with avidity and delight to feast on[6] Dante, Petrarch, and many others. The other critics in your language seem to this day to have no other design than to satisfy[7] their own countrymen, without taking any concern about anybody else. Though I think that they would have provided better for their own reputation, and for the

---

[1] *carry singular freedom of mind.* Use 'libertatem singularis exempli præ se ferre;' and cf. Pliny's words, 'uxor singularis exempli.'

[2] *pass current.* Use 'venditare' for the active 'to pass current;' and cf. Liv. iii. 35, 'per illos so plebi venditare,' much in this sense.

[3] *make the Tuscan language his delight.* Use 'qd in deliciis habero.'

[4] *slightly tinctured,* &c. Cf. Quinc. i. 2, 'litteris leviter im-

butus;' and Hor. Epist. II. ii. 7, 'verna litterulis Græcis imbutus.'

[5] *wetted the tip,* &c. Cf. Cic. de Orat. i. 19, 'quæ isti rhetores ne primoribus quidem labris attigerunt.'

[6] *delight to feast on.* Cf. Cic. ad Att. iv. 10, 'ego hic pascor bibliothecâ Fausti;' and for 'to retire,' use 'se in otium referre,' or 'se a negotiis retrahere.'

[7] *satisfy.* Cf. Cic. ad Att. vi. 1, 'quos libros tibi probari volo.'

glory of the Italian language, if they had delivered their
precepts in such a manner as if it was for the interest of
all men to learn the language.

CXXIV.

Public order rests on two foundations: first, the stability
of the governing body; secondly, the consent and accordance of public opinion with the established government,
not indeed in every particular, which is neither possible
nor even desirable, but in its general tenor.[1] In every age
and country there must be disputes concerning the administration of government; but so long as the foundations of public confidence remain unshaken, the danger is
not great.   Opinions are in perpetual flux and progress: [2]
so long as a government is actuated by the same general
spirit, and feels the necessity of moving in the same direction, no violent convulsions need be feared.   But when
the constitutional powers doubt, vacillate, and conflict with
one another, whilst, at the same time, opinions essentially
hostile to the existing order of things become predominant,[3]
then indeed is the peril imminent.

CXXV.

(CHANCELLOR'S MEDALS, 1825.)

There are two sorts of avarice; the one is but of a
bastard kind,[4] and that is the rapacious appetite of gain,
not for its own sake, but for the pleasure of refunding it [5]
immediately through all the channels of pride and luxury.
The other is the true kind, and properly so called; which
is a restless and unsatiable desire of riches, not for any
further end or use, but only to hoard and preserve and
perpetually increase them.   The covetous man of the first

---

[1] *in its general tenor.* Cf. Tac.
Germ. v., 'terra etsi aliquando
specie differt, in universum tamen,'
&c.

[2] *flux and progress.* Use ' huc
illuc impelli et progredi.'

[3] *opinions become predominant.*
Cf. Liv. ii. 23, ' invidiamque suâ
sponte gliscentem,' &c.

[4] *of a bastard kind.* Use 'parum
legitima.'

[5] *refunding.* Cf. Cic. Philip. ii.
20, ' si hoc est explere quod statim
effundas.'

kind is like a greedy ostrich, which devours any metal ; but it is with an intent to feed upon it, and in effect it makes a shift to digest it.[1] The second is like the foolish chough, which loves to steal money only to hide it. The first does much harm to mankind, and a little good too to some few. The second does good to none ; no, not to himself. The first can make no excuse to God or rational men [2] for his actions. The second can give no reason or colour, not to the devil himself, for what he does ; he is a slave to Mammon [3] without wages. The first makes a shift to be beloved, ay, and envied too,[4] by some people. The second is the universal object of hatred and contempt.

CXXVI.

As soon as the approach of the troops was announced, Cæsar went out to meet them, and ascended his tribunal, which had been erected in a plain before the gates of the city. After distinguishing the soldiers who by their rank or merit deserved a peculiar attention,[5] Julian addressed himself in a studied oration [6] to the surrounding multitude. He celebrated their exploits with grateful applause, encouraged them to accept with alacrity the honour of serving under the eyes of a powerful and liberal monarch, and admonished them that the commands of Augustus required an instant and cheerful obedience. The soldiers, who were apprehensive of offending their general by an indecent clamour, or of belying their sentiments [7] by false and venal acclamations, maintained an obstinate silence, and after a short pause were dismissed to their quarters.

[1] *it makes a shift to digest.* Uso ' nescio quo pacto concoquere.'

[2] *rational men.* Avoid ' rationalis,' a late word. Turn by ' ratione utens,' or ' præditus.'

[3] *a slave to Mammon,* &c. Cf. Sall. Cat., lii. ' domi voluptatibus hic pecuniæ aut gratiæ servitis.'

[4] *and envied too.* ' Invideo,' governing a dative in the active, can only, of course, be used impersonally in the passive. Cf. Cic. do Orat. ii. 51, ' invidetur commodis hominum.'

[5] *deserved peculiar attention.* Cf. Cic. de Orat. i. 54, ' amplissimis honoribus et præmiis decorari.'

[6] *studied oration.* Cf. Cic. ad Att. vi. 9, ' litterularum quæ solent tuæ esse compositissimæ.'

[7] *belie their sentiments.* Use ' sententias veras animi mentiri ;' or cf. Cic. de Amic. xxv., ' simulatio judicium veri adulterat.'

The principal officers were entertained by Cæsar, who professed in the warmest language of friendship his desire and his inability[1] to reward, according to their deserts, the brave companions of his victories. They retired from the feast full of grief and perplexity, and lamented the hardship of their fate, which tore them from their beloved general and from their native country.   GIBBON.

CXXVII.

The Protector, before he opened the campaign, published a manifesto,[2] in which he enforced all the arguments for that measure. He said that Nature seemed originally to have intended this island for one empire :[3] and having cut it off from all communication with foreign nations, and guarded it by the ocean, she had pointed out to the people the road to happiness and security ; that the education and customs of the people concurred with Nature, and by giving them the same language, and laws, and manners, had invited them to a thorough union and coalition ; that fortune had at last removed all obstacles, and had prepared an expedient[4] by which they might become one people, without leaving any place for that jealousy, either of honour or of interests, to which rival nations[5] are naturally exposed : that the crown of Scotland had devolved on a female, that of England on a male ; and happily the two sovereigns, as of a rank so also were of an age the most suitable to each other. That the hostile disposition which prevailed between the nations, and which arose from past injuries, would soon be extinguished, after a long and secure peace had established confidence

---

[1] *his desire and inability,* &c. Turn by ' that he wished, but was not able,' &c.

[2] *published a manifesto.* Cf. De Orat. Dial. ix., ' libellos dispergit;' or turn by ' argumenta per libellos edita confirmare.'

[3] *intended for one empire.* Turn by ' id voluisse ut in unum populum insula conveniret.'

[4] *prepared an expedient.* Cf. Cic. Tusc. i. 14, ' Hercules nunquam ad deos abiisset, nisi eam sibi viam muniisset.'

[5] *to which rival nations,* &c. Use ' obnoxium esse ci rei,' or ' qualis inter æmulos esse solet,' or ' ut inter æmulos.'

between them ; and that the memory of former miseries, which at present inflamed their mutual animosities, would then only serve to make them cherish with more passion a state of happiness and tranquillity so long unknown to their ancestors.   HUME'S *England*.

CXXVIII.

(CLASSICAL TRIPOS, 1848.)

Physicians tell us that there is a great deal of difference between taking a medicine and the medicine getting into [1] the constitution. A difference not unlike which [2] obtains with respect to those great moral propositions which ought to form the directing principles of human conduct. It is one thing to assent to a proposition of this sort ; another, and a very different thing, to have properly imbibed its influence.[3] I take the case to be this ; perhaps almost every man living has a particular train of thought [4] into which his mind falls when at leisure from the impressions and ideas that occasionally excite it ; perhaps also the train of thought here spoken of more than any other thing determines the character.[5] It is of the utmost consequence, therefore, that this property of [6] our constitution be well regulated.

CXXIX.

The popular humours [7] of a great city are a never-failing source of amusement to the man whose sympathies are hospitable [8] enough to embrace all his kind,[9] and who, refined though he may be himself, will not sneer at the

---

[1] *the medicine getting into*, &c. Turn by 'the medicine is thoroughly mixed with the body' (immisceor).

[2] *A difference not unlike which*, &c. Turn by 'quod ferè idem verum est.'

[3] *imbibed its influence*. Cf. Liv. ii. 53, 'tantum certamen animis imbiberant.'

[4] *has a particular train of thought*. Cf. Cic. Epist. iv. 5, 'in eam cogitationem veneris, et nos saepe incidimus.'

[5] *determines the character*. Cf.

Cic. de Fin. iv. 2, 'pars philosophiæ quâ mores conformari putantur.'

[6] *this property of*, &c. Turn by 'that the mind should be well trained in this respect.'

[7] *The popular humours*, &c. Use 'quotidiani plebis sales.'

[8] *whose sympathies are hospitable*, &c. Use 'qui animo adeò benevolo est ut.' &c.

[9] *all his kind*, &c. Cf. Cat. iii., 'quantum est hominum venustiorum ;' and cf. Liv. xxiii. 8, 'per quicquid deorum est.'

humble wit or grotesque peculiarities[1] of the boozing
mechanic, the squalid beggar, the vicious urchin, and all
the motley group of[2] the idle and reckless that swarm in
the alleys[3] and broadways of the metropolis.　He who
walks through a great city to find subjects for weeping,
may find plenty at every corner to wring his heart; but
let such a man walk on his course, and enjoy his grief
alone[4]—we are not of those who would accompany him.
The miseries of us poor earth-dwellers gain no alleviation
from the sympathy of those who merely hunt them out to
be pathetic over them.　The weeping philosopher[5] too
often impairs his eyesight by his woe, and becomes unable
from his tears to see the remedies for the evils which he
deplores.　Thus it will often be found that the man of no
tears is the truest philanthropist, as he is the best phy-
sician who wears a cheerful face[6] even in the worst of
cases.　　　　　　　　　　　　　　　　　　　MACKAY.

CXXX.

Leopold of Anhalt[7] was one of the most eminent generals of his age. · With consummate experience in military
matters, he united a genius well fitted for business.　His
brutal manners excited fear, and his countenance was an
index[8] to his character.　His immoderate ambition hurried
him into every crime to accomplish his object.　He was
a faithful friend, but an irreconcilable enemy, and extremely vindictive[9] to those who were so unfortunate as

[1] *grotesque peculiarities.*　Use
'mores ridiculi.'

[2] *motley group of,* &c.　See note
on 'all his kind.'

[3] *swarm in the alleys,* &c.　Cf.
Cic. pro Cæl. xiv., 'ut viam alienis
viris celebrares;' and De Divin. i.
32, 'vias angiportusque constra-
verat.'

[4] *enjoy his grief alone.*　Cf. Cic.
in Verr. iv. 19, 'clamare cœperunt
sibi ut haberet hæreditatem.'

[5] *The weeping philosopher,* &c.
Turn by 'the philosopher by weeping brings it to pass that his eyesight is impaired;' and cf. Cic. de

Fin. iv. 24, 'hebes est acies oculorum:' also 'porrum aciem oculorum
hebetat.'

[6] *wears a cheerful face,* &c.　Cf.
Cic. ad Att. v. 10, 'hæc ipsa fero
equidem fronte et vultu bellissimè:'
for the next words, cf. 'prope jam
desperatâ salute.' (Cæs.)

[7] *of Anhalt.*　Avoid the simple
genitive in such cases. Turn by an
adjective, or paraphrase.

[8] *his countenance was an index.*
Cf. Cic. in Orat. xviii., 'imago
animi vultus, indices oculi.'

[9] *extremely vindictive.*　Cf. 'virum
inimicitiarum persequentissimum'

to offend him. He was cruel and dissembling. He had a cultivated mind, and could be very agreeable in conversation if he pleased. Grumbkow might be accounted one of the ablest ministers who had appeared for a long time. He was highly polished,[1] easy and engaging in conversation. He understood how to blend the grave and the gay. But this agreeable outside[2] covered a crafty and treacherous heart. His conduct was most dissolute, and his whole character was but a tissue of vices,[3] which rendered him an abomination to all the honest and upright.

CAMPBELL.

CXXXI.

Five-and-twenty years ago, the adventurous traveller on his way to Constantinople suffered many hardships altogether unknown to the traveller of the present year. He was fortunate, if he were not detained for a couple of days at some fording-place in France, in an auberge without windows ;[4] if many unpleasant incidents did not check his progress through Piedmont ; if, on his Mediterranean voyage, under the auspices of a garlic-eating captain, he did not find it absolutely necessary to sleep in top-boots,[5] to preserve his feet from the ravages of enormous ship rats ; if, in short, he did not suffer under calamities too numerous to mention. As regards the rats, let us note that the Genoese admiralty allowed a sou a day[6] for the support of a cat in each ship of war. Arrived at Constantinople, the traveller was troubled for backsheish[7] the instant he arrived at the entrance to the port. The

---

[1] *highly polished.* Cf. Cic. de clar. Orat. xxv., ' vir vitâ omni et victu excultus atque expolitus.'

[2] *But this agreeable outside,* &c. Turn by ' a crafty . . . . was under (suberat) this specious outside ;' and cf. Horace's expression, ' speciosâ fronte decora.'

[3] *a tissue of vices.* Cicero has ' ingurgitare se in vitia ;' which is, perhaps, too strong : uso ' omnibus vitiis tenori ;' or ' affinem esse,'

after Cicero.

[4] *an auberge without windows.* Uso ' hospitium malè fenestratum.'

[5] *sleep in top-boots.* Cf. Juv. iii. 322, ' veniam caligatus in agros ;' or Pers. v. 102, ' navem si poscat sibi peronatus arator.'

[6] *a sou a day.* Use ' binos in diem asses,' as near enough.

[7] *backsheish.* Cf. Cic. in Verr. v. 50, ' ut ad illos fructus arationum corollarium nummorum adderetur.'

captain of the port[1] rowed off to the ship, begged for a gratuity, and, if money were refused, talked about his sick wife, and requested a donation of maccaroni.[2] On landing, the traveller was introduced to the Turkish custom-house officers by an Armenian dragoman. These officers were seated in a row on a divan;[3] each provided with a chibouque[4] and an attendant to serve coffee.

HOUSEHOLD WORDS.

CXXXII.

It will ever be one of the nicest problems for a man to solve, how far he shall profit by the thoughts of other men, and not be enslaved by them. He comes into the world, and finds swaddling-clothes ready for his mind as well as for his body. There is a vast scheme[5] of social machinery set up about him; and he has to discern how he can make it work with and for him, without becoming part of the machinery himself. In this lie the anguish and the struggle of the greatest minds. Most sad are they, having mostly the deepest sympathies,[6] when they find themselves breaking off from communion with other minds. They would go on, if they could, with the opinion around them. But, happily, there is something to which a man owes a larger allegiance[7] than to any human affection. He would be content to go away from a false thing, or quietly to protest against it; but in spite of him the strife in his heart breaks out[8] into burning utterance by word or deed.

FRIENDS IN COUNCIL, Vol. I.

[1] *captain of the port.* Use 'limenarcha.'

[2] *maccaroni.* Cf. Pers. v. 73, 'scabiosâ tesserulâ far possidet.'

[3] *divan.* Use 'hemicyclium.'

[4] *chibouque.* Use 'fumisugium.'

[5] *There is a vast scheme,* &c. Cf. Tac. Hist. i. 20, 'vitiorum instrumenta manerent.'

[6] *having deepest sympathies.* Cf.

Ter. Heaut. I. i. 25, 'homo sum; humani nihil a me alienum puto.'

[7] *owes a larger allegiance.* Cf. Cic. de Off. iii. 34, 'tribuamus aliquid voluptati;' or use 'potius hujus rei rationem habere quàm illius.'

[8] *break out into burning,* &c. Cf. Liv. xl. 35, 'in perniciosam seditionem exarsuri.'

CXXXIII.

One of the most comical [1] sights to superior beings must be to see two human creatures, with elaborate speech and gestures, making each other exquisitely uncomfortable [2] from civility ; the one pressing what he is most anxious that the other should not accept, and the other accepting only from the fear of giving offence [3] by refusal. There is an element of charity [4] in all this too ; and it will be the business of a just and refined nature to be sincere and considerate at the same time. This will be better done by enlarging our sympathy, so that more things and people are pleasant to us, than by increasing the civil and conventional part [5] of our nature, so that we are able to do more seeming with greater skill and endurance. Of other false hindrances to pleasure, such as ostentation and pretences of all kinds, there is neither charity nor comfort in them. They may be got rid of altogether, and no moaning made over them.　　　　FRIENDS IN COUNCIL, Vol. I.

CXXXIV.

(ST. JOHN'S COLLEGE.)

If we can prefer personal merit to accidental greatness, [6] we shall esteem the birth of Tacitus more truly noble than that of kings. He claimed his descent from the philosophic historian whose writings will instruct the last generations of mankind. The senator Tacitus was then seventy-five years of age. The long period of his innocent life was adorned with wealth and honours. He had twice been invested with the consular dignity, and enjoyed with ele-

---

[1] *One of the most comical*, &c. Turn by 'to the gods beholding, it must seem a ridiculous thing that,' &c.

[2] *make each other uncomfortable.* Use 'inter se,' or 'alterum alteri molestias adferre.'

[3] *giving offence.* Cf. Cic. ad Att. xiii. 23, ' mihi majori offensioni sunt possessiunculæ meæ.' Also ' in offensionem cadere.'

[4] *There is an element of charity.* Cf. Cic. de Off. iii. 3, 'in his rebus aliquid probi insit.'

[5] *conventional part.* Turn by ' that part of ourselves which is contained in civil offices.'

[6] *accidental greatness.* Cf. Tac. Hist. i. 49, ' claritas natalium,' &c. ; and for '*last generations*' cf. Tac. Agric. xlvi., 'in æternitate temporum.'

gance and sobriety his ample patrimony [1] of between two and three millions sterling. The experience of so many princes whom he had esteemed or endured, from the vain follies of Elagabalus to the useful vigour of Aurelian, taught him to form a just estimate of the duties, the dangers, and the temptations of their sublime station. [2] From the assiduous study [3] of his immortal ancestor he derived the knowledge of the Roman constitution and of human nature. The voice of the people had already named Tacitus as the citizen the most worthy of empire. The ungrateful rumour reached his ears, and induced him to seek the retirement of one of his villas in Campania. [4] He had passed two months in the delightful privacy of Baiæ, when he reluctantly obeyed the summons of the consul to resume his honourable place in the senate, and to assist the republic with his counsels on that important occasion.

CXXXV.

There is one thing that I should think must often make women very unreasonable and unpleasant companions. Oh, you may both hold up your hands and eyes, but I am not married, and can say what I please! [5] Of course you put on the proper official [6] look of astonishment, and I will duly report [7] it. But I was going to say, that chivalry, [8] which has doubtless done a great deal of good, has also

---

[1] *enjoyed his patrimony,* &c. Cf. Nep. in Att. xiv., ' in sestertio vicies parùm splendidè se gesserit:' and Seneca has 'superfuturum sibi sestertium centies computavit.' In this construction, 'sestertium' is used like a singular noun, and declined: 'vicies' here stands for 'vicies centena millia.'

[2] *sublime station.* Use ' principatus,' or cf. 'summum inter homines fastigium servent.' For the words preceding, notice Livy's phrase, 'res urbanas rusticasque callere.'

[3] *From the assiduous study.* Cf. Cic. ad Att. v. 12, ' meos libros per-

volutas;' or use 'scriptis es deditum esse.'

[4] *one of his villas in Campania.* Cf. Cic. ad Att. i. 6, 'Nos Tusculano ita delectamur.'

[5] *can say what I please.* Cf. Cic. ad Att. i. 12, ' quod in buccam venerit, scribito.'

[6] *put on the official,* &c. Cf. Tac. Hist. i. 82, ' miles compositus in obsequium.'

[7] *I will duly report.* Cf. Tac. Hist. i. 55, 'neque enim erat adhuc cui imputaretur.'

[8] *chivalry.* Use 'Equestris, quam vocant ratio.'

aone a great deal of harm. Women may talk the greatest unreason out of doors, and nobody kindly informs them that it is unreason. They do not talk much before clever men ; and when they do, their words are humoured and dandled,[1] as children's sayings are. Now, I should fancy— mind, I do not want either of you to say that my fancy is otherwise than quite unreasonable [2]—I should fancy that when women have to hear reason at home, it must sound odd [3] to them. The truth is, you know, we cannot pet anything much without doing it mischief. You cannot pet the intellect, any more than the will, without injuring it. Well then, again, if you put people upon a pedestal, and do a great deal of worship around them, I cannot think but the will in such cases must become rather cor- rupted, and that lessons of obedience [4] must fall rather harshly. FRIENDS IN COUNCIL, I. 127.

CXXXVI.

There is no person in that age about whom historians have been more divided, or whose character has been drawn in such opposite colours. Personal intrepidity, military skill, sagacity and vigour in the administration of civil affairs, are virtues which even his enemies allow him to have possessed in an eminent degree. His moral quali- ties are more dubious, and ought neither to be praised nor censured without great reserve [5] and many distinctions. In a fierce age, he was capable of using victory with humanity, and of treating the vanquished with moderation. A patron of learning,[6] which among martial nobles was either unknown or despised. Zealous for religion, to a

---

[1] *humoured and dandled.* Use ' summo obsequio jactari.'

[2] *is quite unreasonable.* Cf. Cic. ad Att. iv. 14, ' quos libros in ma- nibus habeo, ut spero tibi valde probabo.'

[3] *sound odd.* Cf. ' sonare rau- cum, femineum,' &c. ; also ' soli- dum creparo' (Pers. v. 25) ; which last is perhaps too poetical.

[4] *lessons of obedience,* &c. Cf. Suet. in Cæs. liv., ' quanquam nec imperata detrectarent.'

[5] *Without reserve,* &c. Cf. Cic. in Top. xxii., ' quum quæritur quaie quid sit, aut simpliciter quæritur aut comparatè.'

[6] *A patron of learning.* Cf. Cic. de Off. i. 30, ' veritatis cultores.'

H

degree which distinguished him even at a time when pro-
fessions of that kind were not uncommon. His confidence
in his friends was extreme, and inferior only to his liberality
towards them; which knew no bounds. A disinterested
passion for the liberty of his country prompted him to
oppose the pernicious system which the Princes of Lorrain
had obliged the Queen-mother [1] to pursue. On Mary's return into Scotland, he served her with a zeal and affection
to which he sacrificed the friendship of those who were
most attached to his person.

CXXXVII.

But, on the other hand, his ambition was immoderate,[2]
and events happened that opened to him vast projects,
which allured his enterprising genius, and led him to
actions inconsistent [3] with the duty of a subject. His
treatment of the Queen, to whose bounty he was so much
indebted, was unbrotherly and ungrateful. The depend-
ence on Elizabeth, under which he brought Scotland, was
disgraceful to the nation. He deceived and betrayed
Norfolk with a baseness unworthy of a man of honour.
His elevation to such unexpected dignity inspired him
with new passions, with haughtiness and reserve : and
instead of his natural manner, which was blunt and open,
he affected the arts of dissimulation and refinement. Fond,
towards the end of his life, of flattery, and impatient of
advice, his creatures, by soothing his vanity, led him
astray; while his ancient friends stood at a distance, and
predicted his approaching fall. But, amidst the turbulence
and confusion of that factious period, he dispensed justice [4]
with so much impartiality, he repressed the licentious
Borderers with so much courage, and established such uncommon order and tranquillity in the country, that his

[1] *the Queen-mother.* Use 'divi
principis uxor.'
  [2] *immoderate.* Cf. Vell. ii. 33,
'in honoribus appetendis immo-
dicus.'
  [3] *inconsistent with,* &c.   Use

'majora quàm pro cive incepta
moliri,' or 'inire.'
  [4] *he dispensed justice,* &c. Use
'integrum esse in judicando,' or
'æquitate judiciorum uti.'

administration was extremely popular, and he was long and affectionately remembered among the commons by the name of the Good Regent.[1]

ROBERTSON's *Scotland*, II. Book 5.

CXXXVIII.

(CHANCELLOR'S MEDALS, 1842.)

The administration of Valerian was distinguished by a levity and inconsistency ill suited to the gravity of the Roman Censor. In the first part of his reign he surpassed in clemency those princes who had been suspected of an attachment to the Christian faith. In the last three years and a half, listening to the insinuations of a minister addicted to the superstitions of Egypt, he adopted the maxims and imitated the severity of his predecessor Decius. The accession of Gallienus, which increased the calamities of the empire, restored peace to the Church: the Christians obtained the free exercise of their religion,[2] by an edict addressed to the bishops, and conceived in such terms as seemed to acknowledge their office and public character. The ancient laws, without being formally repealed, were suffered to sink into oblivion; and excepting only some hostile intentions, which are attributed to the emperor Aurelian, the disciples of Christ passed above forty years in a state of prosperity, far more dangerous[3] to their virtue than the severest trials of persecution.

CXXXIX.

Cortes receiving his commission with the warmest expressions[4] of respect and gratitude to the governor, immediately erected his standard before his own house, appeared in a military dress, and assumed all the ensigns

---

[1] *by the name of the Good Regent.* Cf. Liv. i. 34, ' puero ab inopiâ Egerio inditum nomen,' where ' Egerio' is the dative by attraction to ' puero.'

[2] *free exercise of their religion.* Cf. Cæs. B. G. vi. 12, ' procurare sacrificia;' and Nep. in Themist.

c. ii., ' procurare sacra;' or Livy, i. 31, ' operatum his sacris.'

[3] *more dangerous to,* &c. Cf. Tac. Hist. i. 15, ' secundæ res acrioribus stimulis animos explorant.'

[4] *with the warmest expressions.* Cf. Liv. v. 7, ' cum amplissimis verbis gratiæ ab senatu actæ esse .

of his new dignity. His utmost influence and activity were exerted in persuading many of his friends to engage in the service, and in urging forward the preparations for the voyage. All his own funds, together with what money he could raise by mortgaging his lands and Indians, were expended in purchasing military stores and provisions, or in supplying the wants of such of his officers as were unable to equip themselves in a manner suitable to their rank. Inoffensive and even laudable as this conduct was, his disappointed competitors were malicious enough to give it a turn to his disadvantage :[1] they represented him as aiming already, with little disguise, at establishing an independent authority[2] over his troops, and endeavouring to secure their respect or love by his ostentatious and interested liberality. They reminded Velasquez of his former dissensions with the man in whom he now reposed so much confidence, and foretold that Cortes would be more apt to avail himself of the power which the governor was inconsiderately putting in his hands, to avenge past injuries[3] than to requite past obligations.

ROBERTSON.

CXL.

"Multis utile bellum" is a well known saying,[4] and there is, unfortunately, some truth in these unpleasant words. But has any one numbered the millions to whom peace is useful? Let us enter into reckonings upon this matter. War may be useful to contractors, armourers, the population of some seaport towns and arsenals, occasionally to certain classes of ship-owners and merchants, and generally to those through whose hands the money raised for war passes. But how very small a proportion[5]

---

[1] *give a turn to his disadvantage.* Use 'vitio dare,' or 'in pejus interpretari.'

[2] *establishing an independent authority.* Cf. Tac. Hist. i. 12, 'ruptâ sacramenti reverentiâ ;' or use 'fidem exuere.'

[3] *to avenge past injuries.* Cf. Tac. Hist. iv. 3, 'tanto proclivius est injuriæ quam beneficio vicem exsolvere.'

[4] *is a well-known saying.* Cf. Cic. de Off. i. 10, 'factum est jam tritum sermone proverbium.'

[5] *small a proportion*, &c. Cf. Juv. iii. 61, 'quota portio fœcis Achaiæ.'

do these people bear to the great bulk of the population! How insignificant and transient are their interests compared with those of the mass of the people!—a mere vanishing quantity,[1] as the mathematician would say. We may also admit that war raises the price of provisions. Is that a benefit to the many? It is not even a benefit in the long run [2] to the producer, whose sure gains are based upon the gradual improvement and permanent well-being of the great masses of the people. That the poorer classes should be able to buy a little more bread, a little more meat, and be able to house and clothe themselves a little better, is of far more importance to the landowner,[3] the corn-grower, the manufacturer, and the merchant, than any fitful gains that may be got out of the disordered state of things which war inevitably produces.

FRIENDS IN COUNCIL, 2d *Series*, I. 88.

CXLI.

(QUEEN'S COLLEGE, OXFORD, 1856.)

Charles came forth from that school [4] with social habits, with polite and engaging manners, and with some talents for lively conversation; addicted beyond measure to sensual indulgence, fond of sauntering and of frivolous amusements, incapable of self-denial and of exertion, without faith in human virtue or human attachment, without desire of renown, and without sensibility [5] to reproach. According to him, every person was to be bought.[6] But some people haggled more about their price than others: and when this haggling was very obstinate and very skilful it was called by some fine name. The chief trick by which clever men kept up the price of their abilities, was

---

[1] *a mere vanishing quantity.* Cf. Lucret. i. 791, 'no res ad nihilum redigantur funditus omnes.'

[2] *in the long run.* Cf. Tac. Germ. i. 6, 'in universum æstimanti,' &c.

[3] *landowner.* Cicero seems to use 'possessor' absolutely in this sense.

[4] *came forth from that school.*

Cf. Cic. Phil. ii. 2, 'te in meam disciplinam tradideris;' and then use 'evado,' to turn out.

[5] *without sensibility,* &c. Cf. Tac. Hist. i. 49, 'famæ non incuriosus.'

[6] *to be bought.* Cf. Sall. Jug. xxxv., 'urbem venalem si emptorem invenerit.'

called integrity. The chief trick by which handsome women képt up the price of their beauty was called modesty. The love of God, the love of country, the love of family, the love of friends, were phrases of the same sort, delicate and convenient [1] synonymes for the love of self. Thinking thus of mankind, Charles naturally cared very little what they thought of him. Honour and shame were scarcely more to him than light and darkness to the blind. His contempt of flattery has been highly commended, but seems, when viewed in connexion [2] with the rest of his character, to deserve no commendation. It is possible to be below flattery [3] as well as above it. One who trusts nobody, will not trust sycophants: one who does not value real glory, will not value its counterfeit.

CXLII.

I purpose to write the history of England from the accession of King James the Second down to a time which is within the memory [4] of men still living. I shall recount the errors which, in a few months, alienated a loyal gentry [5] and priesthood from the House of Stuart. I shall trace the course of that revolution which terminated the long struggle between our sovereigns and their parliaments, and bound up together the rights of the people and the title of the reigning dynasty. I shall relate how the new settlement was, during many troubled years, successfully defended against foreign and domestic enemies: how under that settlement the authority of law and the security of property were found to be compatible [6] with a liberty of discussion and of individual action never before known:

[1] *delicate and convenient*, &c. Cf. Tac. Ann. iv. 19, 'scelera verbis priscis obtegere;' and Ann. i. 10, 'pietatem erga parentem et tempora reipublicæ obtentui sumpta.'

[2] *when viewed in connexion with.* Cf. Tac. Germ. i. 6, 'in universum æstimante.'

[3] *to be below flattery*, &c. Use 'blanditias imparem esse.'

[4] *within the memory of*, &c. Cf.

Cic. de Leg. Man. xviii., 'usque ad nostram memoriam remansit.'

[5] *a loyal gentry.* Cf. Tac. Ann. iv. 55, 'de studio in populum Romanum memorabant.'

[6] *compatible with a liberty*, &c. Turn by 'liberty of doing and speaking . . . increasing (gliscere), provision was made for . . . (cautum est ci rei),' &c.

how from the auspicious union of order and freedom, sprang a prosperity of which the annals[1] of human affairs had furnished no example : how our country, from a state of ignominious vassalage, rapidly rose to the place of umpire[2] among European powers : how her opulence and her martial glory grew together : how by wise and resolute good faith was gradually established a public credit, fruitful of marvels which to the statesmen of any former age would have seemed incredible : how a gigantic commerce[3] gave birth to a maritime power, compared with which every other maritime power, ancient or modern, sinks into insignificance : how Scotland, after ages of enmity, was at length united to England, not merely by legal bonds, but by indissoluble ties of interest and affection : how in America[4] the British colonies rapidly became far mightier and wealthier than the realms which Cortes and Pizarro had added to the dominions of Charles the Fifth : how in Asia, British adventurers founded an empire not less splendid and more durable than that of Alexander.

Macaulay's *History*, I.

CXLIII.

(Trinity College, Dublin, 1859, and Cambridge, 1843.)

The place was worthy of such a trial. Neither military nor civil pomp was wanting. The gray old walls were hung with scarlet. The long galleries were crowded by an audience such as has rarely excited the fears or the emulation of an orator. The culprit was indeed not unworthy of that great presence. He had ruled an extensive and populous country : had made laws and treaties : had sent forth armies : had set up and pulled down princes. And in his high place[5] he had so borne himself, that all

---

[1] *of which the annals*, &c. Cf. Cic. in Cat. i. 7, ‘si hoc post hominum memoriam contigit nemini.’

[2] *rose to the place of umpire.* Turn by ‘increased even to decide the quarrels .... by arbitration (arbitrium).’

[3] *gigantic commerce.* Use ‘mer- caturas copiosas facere,’ for ‘to carry on a vast commerce.’

[4] *America.* Use ‘terræ ad occidentam sitæ,’ or ‘ad Hesperum jacentes.’

[5] *in his high place.* Cf. Nep. Attic. x., ‘modò hi modò illi in summo fastigio essent.’

had feared him, that most had loved him, and that hatred itself could deny him no title to glory except virtue. He looked like a great man,[1] and not like a bad man. A person small and emaciated, yet deriving dignity from a carriage which, while it indicated deference to the Court,[2] indicated also habitual self-possession and self-respect: a high and intellectual forehead: a brow pensive but not gloomy: a mouth of inflexible decision: a face pale and worn, but serene, on which was written as legibly as under the picture in the council chamber at Calcutta,[3] " Mens æqua in arduis : " such was the aspect with which the great proconsul presented himself to his judges.

MACAULAY'S Essays.

CXLIV.

(ST. JOHN'S COLLEGE, 1856.)

The character of Tiberius as described by Tacitus, is a miracle of art. The historian undertook to make us intimately acquainted with a man singularly dark and inscrutable, with a man whose real disposition long remained swathed up in intricate folds[4] of factitious virtues ; and over whose actions the hypocrisy of his youth and the seclusion of his old age threw a singular mystery.[5] He was to exhibit the specious[6] qualities of the tyrant in a light which might render them transparent, and enable us at once to perceive the covering, and the vices which it concealed. He was to trace the gradations by which the first magistrate of a republic, a senator mingling freely in debate, a noble associating with his brother nobles, was transformed into an Asiatic Sultan. He was to exhibit a

---

[1] *looked like a great man.* Cf. Cic. de Off. iii. 4, ' similitudinem speciemque sapientium gerebant.'

[2] *deference to the Court.* Cf. Tac. Hist. i. 17, ' sermo erga patrem reverens.'

[3] *council chamber at Calcutta.* Use ' Indica curia.'

[4] *intricate folds*, &c. Cf. Cic. ad Q. Frat. I. i. 5, ' multis simulatio-num involucris tegitur, et quasi velis quibusdam obtenditur.'

[5] *threw a singular mystery.* Use ' in dubium vocare.'

[6] *to exhibit the specious*, &c. Turn by ' were so to be illustrated as to lie open to the reader, and the deceit as well as the vices be laid bare.'

character distinguished by courage, self-command, and profound policy, yet defiled by all

> "'Th' extravagancy
> And crazy ribaldry of fancy."

He was to mark the gradual effect of advancing age and approaching death on this strange compound [1] of strength and weakness ; to exhibit the old sovereign of the world sinking into a dotage which, though it rendered his appetites eccentric and his temper savage, never impaired the powers of his stern and penetrating mind—conscious of failing strength, raging with capricious sensuality—yet to the last, the keenest of observers, the most artful of dissemblers, and the most terrible of masters.   The task was one of extreme difficulty.   The execution is almost perfect.   EDINBURGH REVIEW.

---

[1] *strange compound*, &c. Cf. Tac.   malaque mixtus ;' and Hist. i. 10,
Ann. vi. 51, 'idem inter bona   'malis bonisque artibus mixtus.'

THE END.

www.ingramcontent.com/pod-product-compliance
Lightning Source LLC
Chambersburg PA
CBHW032151010726
47493CB00008BA/2653